Sweet Tooth

JASMINE NIGHTSHADE

CRIMSON
ROMANCE
F+W Media, Inc.

Published by
Crimson Romance
an imprint of F+W Media, Inc.
10151 Carver Road, Suite 200
Blue Ash, OH 45242. U.S.A.
www.crimsonromance.com

ISBN 10: 1-4405-9660-3
ISBN 13: 978-1-4405-9660-5
eISBN 10: 1-4405-9661-1
eISBN 13: 978-1-4405-9661-2

Cover art © @iStockphoto.com/jonathandowney.

One

Micah Taylor stood in his father's apartment, ignoring the landlord waiting in the doorway. The place smelled of gin and tobacco, old pizza and lo mein, a smell he'd grown up with and had worked hard to forget over the years. One that, despite the fact that Micah had never actually lived in *this* apartment, had apparently followed his father to his latest domicile.

"You want I should stay?" the landlord asked, jingling his keys as if Micah had forgotten he was there.

Micah turned, hot and sweaty from his travels back to his hometown for the first time in three long years. "I'm gonna be awhile."

The landlord frowned. "I only ask because the cleaning crew is on its way and—"

"He's paid up through the end of the month, right?" Micah growled. If there was one thing his father did consistently, Micah knew, it was pay in advance. After that, the aunt who had given Micah his father's current address would be taking over his affairs. There were debts to pay, he understood, and no will, so ... he wasn't expecting much in the way of an inheritance. He supposed closure would be enough, which was why he had deigned to set foot back in Fiesta again—let alone his father's apartment—in the first place.

The landlord blushed and stared down at his feet. "Well yeah, sure, but when we spoke on the phone yesterday you made it sound like you'd just be stopping by to pay your respects."

Micah dragged the backpack from his shoulder and let it slide onto his father's easy chair, kicking up a fresh wave of beer and potato chip fumes. "That's right. I had a lot of respect for my father, so it might take awhile."

The landlord nodded, still lingering in the doorway. "Okay, sure. I get that. Fathers and sons, that's a special bond, right? All

I'm saying is, are we talking a few hours' worth of respect here? Or a few days, or…what?"

Micah smiled. At least the landlord was consistent. He and his old man had probably gotten along like gangbusters. "I need a cold shower and a black suit, mister. After that, I'm gone. Gimme an hour or two to pay my respects. Can you do that much for me?" Micah didn't think he'd need that much time, but if he got the landlord out of his hair for a few extra minutes, all the better.

The old man nodded eagerly, then paused, admiring the living room cluttered with furniture, walls covered in artwork. "You don't want none of this?"

Micah reached for the door. "Hell no," he said, slamming it in the landlord's face. The sound echoed through the cheap apartment, sending dust bunnies into hiding and, from the sounds of his slippered feet in the hallway, the landlord running. He felt bad for the old man, but he couldn't help it.

Micah had said he'd respected his father; he never said he *loved* him.

Fact was, he and his dad had baggage—whole freight cars full of it. Baggage Micah had assumed they'd unpack one day, maybe over a cold beer at one of his dad's favorite bars, hashing out the misdeeds of their sordid pasts, walking out of the darkness into the light, finally unburdened and free to start anew.

Now that would never happen. A stroke, sudden and swift, had seen to that. He had meant to reach out to the old man over the years, once the pain of that one night so long ago had festered and, if not entirely healed, scabbed over somewhat. Maybe the old man had meant to reach out to him. Now Micah would never know.

Micah sighed and went to the fridge, knowing there'd be a cold six pack inside—and not much else. He wasn't disappointed. He grabbed one, ignoring the rest of the house and drifting into the bathroom, stripping off his damp, sticky clothes along the way.

It had been a long bus ride from the Prestige Art Institute in Atlanta. Long, hot, boring, and dusty. He had fantasized that he might spot some sexy stranger along the way, following him into the men's room for a quick tug and chug but, alas, there had been mostly single ladies or retirees, neither very much interested in the brooding ex-art student in the back.

The bathroom was small and dirty; water stains surrounded Micah as he stood beneath cold water that never quite warmed. That was fine with him—he had enough body heat from the seventeen-hour trip to spare.

His father's death, and the summons to attend his funeral—ignored until Micah's conscience could ignore it no longer—had proved a tipping point in his life. Rousing him from a weeks'-long slumber after being asked to leave art school, he had been drifting through a kind of dream state: unbelieving, uncertain, unsure.

The decision to visit his father's gravesite had proved a fateful one, pulling him out of his self-imposed sabbatical and forcing him to confront his oldest, and fiercest demons. Now that he was here, he felt no closer to relief than he had when he'd first bought a bus ticket for the long sojourn home.

He dried off with a stiff towel his father had probably used, and wasn't sure how to feel about that. He got rid of it quickly, his short hair still damp as he padded, naked, back into the living room. He hadn't brought much with him, just what he'd worn on the bus and a few fresh pairs of underwear and socks shoved to the bottom of his backpack. He was fine borrowing a suit from the old man, but not his drawers.

Standing up from tugging on his boxers, Micah noted the old record player in the corner. "Jesus," he murmured, recognizing it from his youth and unable to resist. He let his fingers drift through the old album covers, settling on Miles Davis and smiling despite himself as the rich, chaotic tones filled the smelly old room.

There had been good times growing up, before Micah's mother passed from cancer when he was but a boy—and even afterward, when it was just him and his father trying to make their way through the wreckage that remained of their lives together and apart. Barbecues and cookouts, card games and old movies on TV, and, always, music. Jazz, mostly. Blues, whenever his father bought a fifth instead of a pint.

But the good times were too few and far between, and even a shared love of good music wasn't enough to drown out the shouting, the accusations and, ultimately, the dismissal.

Micah drifted toward his father's room, finding a cheap black suit, cheaper black socks, and polished black shoes in the closet. He tugged them on, studying the mostly fitting getup in a dusty full length mirror in the corner. Smirking ironically at the church suit, Micah stuck his hands in the pockets, striking an uncertain pose. He felt bills, several of them. Dragging them out, he found tens and twenties, two of each.

Returning to the closet, Micah mined the half-dozen jackets hanging there to discover a hidden stash of loose bills, some crumpled, some folded, his father's version of a piggy bank, he supposed. Micah smirked, pocketing the cash and wondering if that was why the landlord was so eager to return. He felt naked, somehow, without a tie, but couldn't find one anywhere.

He was turning from the room when he noticed a framed picture on the dresser by the drawer. He paused, picking it up with suddenly trembling hands. It was of his parents, both of them, so young and striking in their differences and similarities. It wasn't a wedding picture, or even a studio portrait. It was a casual snapshot, shot somewhere relaxing, Micah's mother—white and prissy in a sundress—clinging to his father, ebony skin dark in the sun as they shared a quiet moment captured by a family member or friend's camera.

Micah had known so little of his mother, it might have been his father hugging a stranger. And seeing his father in happier times only made him feel guilty about the years that had passed since they'd last spoken.

Back in the hall, he saw one last room, past the bathroom, the door closed. Curious, thinking he might find a vast tie collection lurking just beyond the door, he opened it—and found a museum instead.

It was his room, almost just as he'd left it after his father kicked him out the night of high school graduation three years ago. That hadn't happened here, in this rundown fleabag apartment, but his father must have moved it here, either recreating it by memory or dumb, blind luck.

Micah's artwork hung from the walls, amateurish but inspired, framed and orderly all around the room. The bed had the same sheets and comforter; the same wicker chair sat in the corner, beneath the good lamp, where he'd sit up long after his father passed out at night, sketchbook in hand, drawing furiously until he passed out, too—drunk from art instead of beer or gin.

And there, against the wall, his old skateboard. A little battered, a little bruised, but there just the same. It even had the same stupid peace sign sticker in the middle, frayed but permanent now, he supposed. Micah grabbed it, shut the door behind him, and didn't look back.

Skateboard under his arm, he snatched his backpack off the easy chair and reached for the door. Half-in, half-out, he paused, returning to the kitchen. The money feeling greasy and unclean in his coat pocket, he slid it in the fridge next to the six-pack, twisting off one last beer in exchange.

Two

Cash Callahan was knee deep in the sugarplum display when something even sweeter walked through the door of his candy store, the Sweet Tooth.

"Micah?"

Micah Taylor stood just inside the doorway, looking shabby chic in an ill-fitting black suit over a crisp white shirt, the collar open with no tie. He held a skateboard under one arm, the same one he'd ridden back in school, down to the same stupid peace symbol sticker on the deck. His soft brown skin was aglow, looking radiant, slick, and sexy as hell. Soft eyes peered back at Cash uncertainly, before widening with recognition.

"Cash?" he cried out, coming the rest of the way into the store and letting the door swing shut behind him. "What the hell, man?"

Cash shrugged, not sure how to reply. Instead he came out from the window display, wiped his hands on his green and white Sweet Tooth apron, and went to shake Micah's hand.

In that moment, the two of them intimate and still in the empty store, Cash felt a flood of emotions surge through his body. Seeing his former classmate was a flashback he'd neither expected, nor was prepared for. He'd thought he'd put his feelings for Micah, never voiced to anyone but himself, far behind him.

He had certainly worked hard enough to, over the three years since they'd last seen one another, creating his "straight" life in Fiesta as carefully as he regarded his finances, his health, or any other important aspect of his life. He'd made peace with small town life, even relative celibacy. Or, at least, he thought he had. Clearly, the thumping of his heart and pounding of blood rushing through his ears told him all was not forgotten—not by a long shot.

Micah went to shake his hand, but at the last second seemed to change his mind and wrapped Cash in a warm, velvet hug instead.

It was an electric sensation that both captivated and alarmed him. They had never even shaken hands before, and suddenly here they were, locked in an embrace straight out of one of Cash's most secret, devout, and erotic fantasies. He smelled like mothballs, sunshine, and sweat—a heady mixture that made Cash wish the hug would never end. But it did, only too soon, and Cash leaned back against the nearby display counter to admire his old classmate in more ways than one.

"Look at you," he said. Micah was long, lean, and limber, even in the baggy black suit. His hair was shorter than Cash remembered it—sexy, sleek, and framing the same chiseled face, caramel in color and glowing from the sun. "What are you up to these days?" That face darkened quietly in reply to Cash's question.

Looking around the store nervously, Micah scratched his head, an old nervous habit he'd had since they were younger. "Listen, I don't want to bring the reunion down or anything, but I'm on my way to dad's gravesite and wanted to bring some candy with me."

Cash literally slapped his forehead, feeling lower than low. "Oh man, talk about putting your foot in your mouth. I was so sorry when I heard the news…"

Micah stiffened subtly, waving a dismissive hand. "No biggie," he said, avoiding Cash's eyes. "I'm late for the funeral myself. By a few weeks."

They shared a nervous laugh, mostly humorless, Cash uncertain of what to say next. Eager to fill the awkward silence, he jerked his thumb to the left.

"You know there's a florist a few stores down," he said. "Might be a little more appropriate than lollipops and gumballs, you know?"

Micah gave him a deadpan grin. "My old man wasn't much for flowers," he said. "And I know he'd rather have me bring him a pint of something from the liquor store around the corner, but

I wouldn't feel right doing that. I know he had a sweet tooth, so when I saw this place…"

"He sure did," Cash said. When Micah's face darkened once more, Cash explained, "He used to come in here from time to time, looking for a sugar fix."

Micah grunted. "Probably when he was trying to kick the hard stuff. He always wanted sweets when he wasn't drinking booze."

"At least he tried to kick, though, right?" Cash offered. Micah snorted, then said no more. "Anyway," Cash continued, "he got all kinds of stuff over the years, but usually came back to spice drops. You want a bag?"

Micah nodded, visibly relaxing somewhat, as if perhaps comforted by the story. "I never knew that about him. I always just figured he picked up a bag of whatever was handy at the liquor store."

Cash busied himself behind the sales counter, scooping a generous helping of spice drops into a plastic Sweet Tooth bag before wrapping it tight.

"I'm not saying he was a regular customer," Cash said, "but he came in often enough for me to remember the spice drops part." Cash put the plastic candy bag in one of the fancier handled bags he usually reserved for holidays or VIP customers. In a way, seeing Micah again after so many years kind of qualified as both. He held it in his hand awkwardly, before offering it to Micah. Micah smiled gratefully, the bag dangling from two long fingers as he went to reach for his wallet.

Cash held up a hand. "Don't even think about it," he said. "I missed the funeral, too. It's the least I can do."

Micah's eyes held something far more than gratitude, making him look even sadder in his too big suit. "You're going there now? The cemetery, I mean?"

Micah merely nodded, wearing that same sad expression.

"Let me go with you, man," Cash insisted, already reaching behind his back to untie his apron.

Micah blanched and waved his hand, as if that was a really bad idea. "No," he said. "I couldn't ask you to do that, man."

Cash grinned. "You're not asking me, remember? I asked *you*. And I'm going, period." Before Micah could protest any further, Cash stepped behind the sales counter and poked his head over the half door that led into the stockroom.

Surprising the gawky teenager reading a surf magazine in the break room, he said, "Benjy, I'm out for the rest of the day. Cover the store for me?" When Benjy frowned, putting the magazine down, Cash sweetened the deal. "Don't give me that hangdog look. Just take twenty dollars out of the petty cash drawer for your troubles."

Suddenly, Benjy beamed, and Cash's guilt over asking the kid to man the store on his own dissolved like a coating of sugar on a spice drop the minute it hit your tongue. Reaching behind the cash register for his own long board, he slid it under his arm and grabbed Micah by the collar.

"Let's go," he said, opening the door for his former classmate. Micah stood there, looking from Cash to the break room door.

"Can you do that?" he asked.

Cash winked, talking him the rest of the way out of the door and out into the midday sunlight. "I can do anything I want, Micah. That's what happens when you're the boss."

Three

The setting sun set the sky ablaze, filling the air around them with streaks of blue, pink, orange, and black. Sitting next to Cash on the beach, Micah watched it with a combination of awe and déjà vu. Florida sunsets had always been one of his favorite things to paint. Many were a masterpiece unto themselves, and he hadn't realized how much he'd missed them until he saw one for the first time in years.

Then again, the company didn't hurt, either.

Cash seemed to notice, nudging him playfully in his ribs. "You act like you've never seen a sunset before."

"Just been a while since I've seen one from a front row seat," Micah murmured. "That's all."

Cash nodded. "Probably looks a little different from your dorm room in Atlanta," he teased. Micah snorted, leaning farther back as his long, brown fingers swam in the sand.

"I dropped out of school last semester," he confessed.

"No shit?" Cash reached for the six pack between them, cracking open another beer. Micah shrugged, about to reach for one as well, when he found Cash offering him his instead. He was touched by the gesture, as he been touched by every sweet thing Cash had done since he had walked through the door of his candy store earlier that afternoon.

In fact, seeing Cash had put Micah's brief sojourn back home into a tailspin. He had been planning on spending no more than a day or two in tiny Fiesta, Florida, then moving on to South Beach where his pal Jason, an ex-classmate from art school, ran a big advertising agency. Micah had called him before leaving Atlanta and, once his old pal learned he'd be back in Florida, said the job as head of the graphics design department was his—*if* he wanted it. All Micah had to do was get there by the end of the month when the position was due to be filled.

Seeing Cash had changed all that. Micah could hardly believe that out of all the candy stores in all of Florida, he'd walked into his old classmate's. While he had never confessed his love for Cash back in high school, that didn't diminish its passion or strength—even after all these years.

He'd thought he had forgotten it, or at least suppressed it. But seeing Cash again had brought him right back to senior year, sitting in the back of the one class they shared together—World Cultures—and feverishly sketching Cash's young, flawless face. Not that Cash would have ever noticed. Though Micah yearned for the long, lanky redhead, the two had never spoken, let alone hung out. He was a fantasy, nothing more, a beautiful sunset to be sketched and savored from afar.

Micah had burned through many a sketchbook that semester, trying to get the sketch just right. Closer and closer he got, until slowly he perfected the square jaw, the lean cheeks, the cute pug nose, his soft green eyes, and even his feathery red eyelashes. But each feature he perfected only made the rest look flawed. And so another drawing would bite the dust, another page crumpled and torn and tossed into the wastebasket in the back of class.

It was only during the last week of senior year that Micah finally saw fit to finish a sketch and not throw it away. Never one to tout his own work, even Micah had to admit the drawing was beautiful. Then again, so was his subject. He had meant to present it to Cash at the graduation bonfire that night, but his father had interfered with that plan.

Micah was usually so careful about hiding his sketches, particularly the ones of Cash, which could only be seen as flattering, even adoring. While Micah had readied himself for graduation, lingering in the shower over secret, unrequited fantasies of Cash, Ezra Taylor had gone into his son's room to put a graduation gift on his pillow.

He'd found instead the cherished sketch, Cash's face so lovingly captured onto a poster size sheet of paper. He was still staring at it in shock when Micah emerged from the shower, clinging loosely to the towel around his waist. To say that that father and son had had words that day would be an understatement of cataclysmic proportions.

In no uncertain terms, Ezra Taylor had not only kicked his son out of the house, but disowned him altogether. Micah barely remembered throwing on some clothes and dashing from the apartment that day. Forget graduation, to say nothing of the bonfire and the moment he'd hoped to have with Cash. He used the cash he'd brought along with him to buy a pint of rum with his fake ID, drinking it under the pier until he passed out.

He waited until he knew his father would be at work the next morning to creep back into the apartment, pack a few things and grab his life savings from the coffee can in his underwear drawer, and head off to Atlanta where he had a full scholarship at Prestige Art Institute starting that fall. He stayed at the Y for less than a week before talking his guidance counselor into letting him attend summer classes and thus stay on campus.

He'd never looked back, at least not until hid nosy aunt had tracked him down and told him of his father's death earlier that month. Now here he was, back in Fiesta, peering at Cash and wondering why fate had brought them together once more.

"Thanks," he said, taking the beer from Cash's hand. Their fingers touched only briefly, and yet it had a sudden an immediate effect on Micah's nervous system, temporarily shutting it down so that he couldn't move. Cash either didn't notice the temporary mental reboot or didn't care, smiling at him curiously until Micah had to yank the beer away in shame. Cash opened a fresh one for himself before leaning back in the sand, his hand coming dangerously close to Micah's.

They drank for a sip or two, until Cash asked, "So why'd you drop out of art school?"

Micah shrugged. "Long story," he said, not wanting to go into the sordid details of the older art professor he'd had an affair with and who, when caught, used his connections to escape any of the resulting fallout while Micah took the heat. Not only was his affair with the teacher against school rules, but ultimately it had cost him his scholarship—no more classes, no more books, no more meals at the commissary, no more dorm room.

It wasn't the disciplinary action that upset him so much, as the betrayal. He hadn't been prepared to be discarded by a lover so easily, and the experience had left him shaken.

He'd spent the rest of that semester bouncing from friend's house to friend's house, crashing on couches, watching cartoons, smoking grass, and generally getting into trouble until his aunt had tracked him down. Even then, the old wounds prevented him from racing farther south to make his dad's funeral on time.

He wasn't going to come at all, but Micah sensed that if he could somehow lay his father to rest, then he could rest in peace as well. The long, tense day hadn't quite provided the closure he'd been looking for, but here he was just the same.

"Long story, huh?" Cash asked, nudging him once more. Micah turned to face him, smiling apologetically. "Maybe you'll tell me someday."

"Maybe," Micah teased, doubting it somehow. After all, did he really want Cash to know the sordid details of why he'd had to leave art school? Did he even want Cash to know he was gay? After all these years, what good would it do? Especially if he only had a few days to stick around.

They had spent nearly two hours at the gravesite, saying nothing, sitting on a marble bench staring at Ezra's tombstone. It was plain, unadorned, and cheap, but a brass plaque on the bottom told Micah the city of Fiesta had paid for it, and that brought him some peace.

Cash nudged Micah once more. "You think we'll go to hell for eating some of your dad's spice drops?"

Micah laughed despite himself, a far too rare sound these days. "I look at it this way," he reasoned aloud. "It's as if we shared a snack with the old man. That's not a sin, is it?"

"You're asking me?" Cash sat up, wriggling his half empty beer can.

Micah followed suit, until they sat knee to knee on the cheap beach towel they'd bought with the beer at Bob's Bodega on Sunset Street. "Thanks for coming today," he said, tempted to reach out and cover Cash's knee with his hand.

Cash shrugged. "I couldn't let you do something like that alone."

Micah nodded gratefully. "I'd never been to a cemetery before," he confessed.

Cash grinned despite the grim subject matter. "Me either."

Micah took a sip of beer, shaking his head. "I always thought we'd have more time."

"Your dad probably did, too."

Micah wasn't sure if it was the beer or the occasion that had him feeling so melancholy. Either way, he'd been unprepared for the emotional day. He cleared his throat, avoiding Cash's eyes. "Did he ever say anything about me? I mean those times he came into your store?"

"All the time," Cash said so confidently, so blatantly, it had to be a lie.

Micah shoved him playfully, grateful for the gesture just the same. "You're full of shit!"

Cash snorted, raising his hands in surrender. "He honestly didn't say much of anything."

Micah nodded. "Talking wasn't really his thing."

Cash smirked. "That's an understatement."

There were two beers left; Micah lifted them both by the plastic six-pack holder. He took one off, opened it, and handed it to Cash. Opening the other for himself, he put their empties in the plastic shopping bag from the bodega nearest the boardwalk. He'd forgotten how quickly the sun set in Fiesta; the sky was now dark save for a half-moon glowing gently overhead.

Cash had never looked more radiant, or sexy. Even now, three years after graduation, he still looked like the high school senior in Micah's sketch. Micah wondered idly where the drawing had gone after he rushed out of the apartment that night. Probably straight down the shitter where his father thought it belonged.

The beach was deserted now—not even the most diehard surfers braved the waves in the dark. If only he had the courage to just lean forward, seize the moment, and press his lips against Cash's. But it felt like high school all over again: Micah too afraid to show his feelings, and Cash straight and uninterested in Micah that way.

"You got a place to stay for the night?" Cash asked as they reluctantly finished their beers. Micah shook his head, too embarrassed to admit he'd probably just crash under the boardwalk for the night.

Cash seemed to sense it and, standing abruptly, reached down for his hand and dragging Micah up off the towel. "You can crash at my place for as long as you need."

When Micah hesitated, unsure how to respond, Cash jerked an eager thumb over his shoulder. "Come on," he said, making it clear he wasn't taking no for an answer. "It's just up the street on Seagull Lane."

Micah nodded, reaching for the beach towel as Cash grabbed the bag full of empties. It clattered and clanked as they walked to the nearest trashcan.

"Just for a few nights," Micah said in reply. "I've got a job waiting on me in South Beach and I don't want to blow it."

"Something art related, I hope?" Cash asked, assuming an almost protective tone.

Micah chuckled. "If you consider staring at a graphics design program for eight hours a day artistic, I suppose."

Cash shrugged, dumping the bag in the can and leading Micah up the deserted stretch of sand.

They walked in silence for a while, side-by-side, so close their hips occasionally brushed up against one another's. It took every ounce of willpower Micah had not to simply reach over and grab Cash's hand. Instead he watched Cash approach a small wooden gate leading up to a small flight of stairs that led to a humble beach cottage.

They paused at the gate, and Micah grinned at his host. "One thing is troubling me," he said, the sandy beach towel tossed over one shoulder.

Cash arched one ginger eyebrow and asked, "Yeah, what's that?"

"How did you know it was my old man in the candy store?"

Cash blushed, before looking briefly away. When he turned back to face him, he said, "I saw him pick you up after the art show one year."

Micah was impressed. "I didn't know you liked art."

Cash winked, reaching for the gate. "There's a lot you don't know about me, Micah. But maybe, if you stick around long enough, you might find out."

Four

Cash couldn't sleep, tossing and turning in his double bed, watching the moonlight creep across the floor as the hours passed in fits and starts. It was like graduation night all over again. He'd waited all senior year, gathering up his courage to tell Micah how he felt. Every day, hearing Micah scrabble away on that damn sketch pad in the back of World Cultures class, Cash told himself this would be the day—the day he finally worked up the courage to ask to see one of his drawings. And every day, the bell would ring, he'd turn around, see Micah peering back at him curiously… and he'd chicken right the fuck out. He'd had no idea at the time that Micah had been back there drawing him. Things might have been different if he had, but how… Cash wasn't sure.

Day after day passed like that, until finally senior year had come to an end. No more World Cultures class. No more Micah, sketching away feverishly in the back of class. No more chances but one: the bonfire after graduation that night.

He'd "borrowed" a pint of rum from his mom's liquor cabinet, stowing it under his robe all through graduation and sipping it by the fire, waiting, anxiously waiting, for Micah to show up. The later it got, the more he drank, and the more elaborate—even erotic—Cash's imaginary confession became. And yet, it was all for naught.

Micah never showed after all and, drunk and horny, poor Cash had finally given Susie Wannamaker what she'd been after all year: his virginity. It was all he could do to get it up in the back of her father's Buick, let alone not scream out Micah's name when, after one long sweaty hour, he finally came.

Unaware that he had been numb the entire time, Susie thought him the perfect lover, creeping into his bed time and time again that long, hot summer before she went away to college in the fall. He'd succumbed every time, not wanting to hurt her feelings, not ready to come out just yet, and closing his eyes the whole time, imagining Micah's soft, wet lips on his own each time they kissed. Pretending it was Micah's mouth wrapped around his cock every time she blew him. Fantasizing it was Micah lying there, face down in the bed each time he rode her sweet, wet hole in the middle of the dark, damp night. He never thought she'd noticed; she'd never said a thing.

That is until they ran into each other a few summers later at the movie theater. She was home to attend her sister's wedding and had snuck out for a little sci-fi double feature before she went home the next day. They sat in the dark in the back of an empty theater, munching popcorn, sharing a bag of Red Vines while vampire astronauts battled werewolves on Mars.

Sitting awkwardly on the trunk of her car in the parking lot afterward, she had leaned in for a soft, dry kiss. He returned it, dutifully as ever, until she pushed him away playfully, giggling.

"What's so funny?" he had asked.

She had shrugged, and finally confessed. "I just wanted to see if you'd still go through with the charade." When he'd replied with a blank stare, she explained that she'd known all along. From that very first time.

"How?" he'd asked, thinking he'd hidden it so well and disappointed that he'd hurt her feelings. "It was the way you kept your eyes closed the whole time," she confessed. "Every time. No guy I've ever been with before or since did that, Cash, except you."

Suddenly, it had all come pouring out. All of it. Not just Micah, but what he'd known since junior high school, hiding his wet boners from the other boys in the locker room shower. He had never told a soul before that night, and hadn't told anyone since. How could he, in a conservative little town like Fiesta, where despite the shimmering surf babes and stoned surfers at every beach access, the churches still outnumbered the surf shops two to one? And who would he tell? He'd had few friends in high school, and fewer since. And the ones he'd had never suspected his attraction to other men, and would have ragged on him for it, making him the butt of every "fag" or "queer" joke for the next four years. He'd learned early on what the folks at school, and in town, thought of anyone different, and had wanted no part of it.

It might have been different if Micah had ever noticed him, let alone returned his affections. He might have risked ridicule and shame to have even one date with his fantasy lover. But barring that? What was the upside? Instead he'd said nothing, to no one.

There had been no need to, not really. His parents never cared who he dated, male or female, young or old. They never asked why he didn't go to prom, or never had a girlfriend or even posters of hot, half-naked chicks on the walls of his room. Then again, they never cared about anything he did, for the most part. Not that they were neglectful, just … absent. Absent from his interests, absent from his swim meets, from his hobbies, from his life. Their divorce his freshman year of high school had been a disruption, but hardly a surprise.

Dad had split for LA with his yoga instructor, and his mom stayed behind to manage the real estate office they'd owned together for as long as Cash could remember. He'd worked nights, weekends, and summers doing property management for the many investment properties his mother had received as part of her settlement in the divorce.

When he graduated high school, his mom gave him a choice: she would pay for him to go to State for up to four years, a nearly $100,000 commitment at the time. Or, she would gift him one of her commercial properties worth equal or lesser value. A born entrepreneur, Cash had quickly opted for the property. However, the only one in his price range at the time was the little, moldy used bookstore she'd come into possession of after the owner defaulted on his loan.

It had sat idle for years and Cash figured he was doing his mom a favor by taking it off her hands. She agreed, and offered to loan him the extra ten grand they both knew it would take to turn the smelly old bookstore into the only candy store in Fiesta, Florida.

While his fellow classmates, including Susie and Micah, went off to pursue their dreams, Cash stayed behind, working long days and long nights painting and stuccoing and tiling and sawing and cleaning and ordering and stocking until the Sweet Tooth was finally open for business, just in time for Halloween.

He never looked back, and neither had his mom, slowly selling off her properties in Fiesta one by one until she had enough stockpiled to retire for good in her vacation beach house in Costa Rica. Now she happily mothered by phone, or more often than not mothered by text, and the closest they got to warm and fuzzy family time was the Christmas cards they exchanged each December.

He was surprisingly unaffected by the move, having already felt orphaned for most of his life. In many ways, Cash skipped the normal period of adjustment between high school and college, or even work life. No partying or hooking up, no dating—men or women. He stayed frozen in time, gliding under the radar, his life after high school really not much different than those four long years.

Under the watchful gaze of his fellow townsfolk, Cash ignored his most fervent desires and focused instead on how he might fill his days to the point where no thoughts of men, Micah or otherwise, might squeeze in. Now he worked and lived as an adult, for the most part, burying his sexual frustrations in eighty-hour work weeks and Internet porn.

To suddenly have another man in his cozy beach cottage, let alone Micah himself, had found Cash's peaceful world not just turned upside down but inside and out. Tired of tossing and turning, he rose at last, realizing it was futile to even try to go back to sleep anymore.

Instead he traded his damp, sticky boxer shorts for a pair of baggies and crept out of his room. Careful to avoid the creaky floorboards in the hallway, Cash noticed Micah's door slightly ajar. His heart seized, thinking perhaps his sexy houseguest might be lying in bed, tossing and turning and thinking of him as well.

He imagined the scenario, as fanciful as any other he'd had over the years, in which he pressed open the guest room door, found Micah lying in his bed, caramel skin aglow beneath a sliver of moonlight waiting for him to approach.

Instead he saw the bed still made, the spare change of clothes Cash had loaned him still folded pristinely on the chair in the corner. Shrugging, he turned and crept into the kitchen, another fantasy forming, where Micah stood, his body bathed in the light of the open fridge.

Strike two, Cash thought to himself, finding the kitchen as empty as the guest bedroom. It was Monday, or would be once the sun came up in a few hours. Monday was Cash's "float" day at the store, the one day a week he was free to come and go as he pleased thanks to hiring enough part-time help to always have the store covered. Figuring a beer couldn't hurt, and might even relax him enough to go back to sleep, he reached for the fresh six-pack in the fridge—and found it gone.

That little stinker, he thought to himself, grinning and grabbing a towel from the peg by the front door. He found Micah, or his discarded boxer shorts at least, lying on the sand not far from his back gate. Only two beers remained of the six-pack Micah had snagged from the fridge. Beyond it, pristine footsteps led into the sea.

Cash followed them with his eyes, finding a gleaming, glowing, radiant form frolicking in the sea. His heart fluttered as the towel slipped from his fingers, the beer suddenly forgotten. Instead he stepped from his flip-flops and trod quietly toward the white froth that sizzled upon the shore.

Micah was beaming, waving him in, a totally different creature from the somber, hesitant stud who'd sat on the beach with him earlier, damp and dour in his big black suit. Now he looked like a creature of the sea, waist buried in the waves, bare chest wet and supple.

The water was warm this time of year, and Cash crept into the waves as if stepping into his own private bathtub. The waves were never big to start with, but even less so on this night. Micah stood in the soft, gleaming stretch of ocean between the gently rolling waves yet to form and those crashing to shore.

Cash approached him cautiously, if eagerly. In the gentle ebb and flow of the ocean current, he could glimpse from time to time Micah's damp, curly thatch of rich black pubic hair that glistened in the moonlight. Drawing his eyes up Micah's body, he feasted on his long thin belly, his lean, hairless chest, and dark brown nipples. He had broad shoulders and long, thin arms and tender fingers reaching out to welcome him.

Micah beamed as they stood in the gently rolling surf. "Welcome, my fellow insomniac!"

"What's gotten into you?" Cash chuckled breathlessly. "Besides most of my six pack, that is?"

Micah shook his head. "I'm not drunk on beer, man. I just never went skinny dipping in high school."

Cash nodded, waiting for what might come next.

"I guess I'm making up for lost time."

Cash felt his belly flutter, the surreal moment and Micah's beauty giving him a sense of confidence he didn't really have. Licking his lips, already salty from the surf, his eyes met Micah's. Voice hoarse, he asked, "What else didn't do in high school that you'd like to make up for?"

Micah's mouth fell open at the obvious line. Cash regretted it the moment it was out of his mouth, but he also knew it was a chance he'd had to take. He couldn't be sure if Micah was gay or not, and frankly no longer cared. Let Micah splash him with water, punch him in the face, or knee him in the balls with disgust if he wanted; Cash didn't care. He'd been a pussy for longer than he cared to admit and if he couldn't hit on Micah when he was standing in front of him, naked, wet, and gleaming in the deserted sea, when else would he be able to?

But Micah just smirked and splashed him playfully, the effort lifting his body slightly so that Cash could glimpse the base of his shimmering cock. "Are you asking me, Cash? Or are you asking yourself?"

"A little of both, I suppose."

Micah grinned and, amazingly, in an unmistakable gesture that surprised him, reached out to clasp Cash's fingers. There was a jolt of power, a surge of electricity, and the flood of relief. This was happening. He. Micah. Right now, in this moment. He wasn't imagining it; it was really, finally happening! What's more, it was mutual. Micah's smile was brighter than the moon high above as he drew Cash closer in the rolling sea.

"I only have one regret from high school," he confessed, fingers tight in Cash's own.

Breathlessly, Cash grunted, "Yeah, what's that?" Micah licked his lips, slick and full beneath the moonlight.

"Just this," he murmured, pulling Cash the rest of the way in. Their lips met and, despite the gently rolling waves, stayed glued to one another's. Micah's hand slid around the small of Cash's back to draw him closer, until at last they were chest to chest and belly to belly.

Cash's head swam, and it wasn't just the rolling of the sea. It was a surreal moment, made only more so by the very public setting. It wasn't the first time he'd gone night swimming, but it *was* the first time he'd gone night swimming with a naked man, who he was kissing, in the middle of the sea, after pining away for him for nearly six years.

At last he sputtered away, breathless and panting, heart pounding so fast he thought the whole town of Fiesta might hear it.

"Micah, I…" Their eyes met and, before Micah's could fill with doubt, Cash kissed him again.

"I don't…" They held a conversation, chaotic and mad, between feverish kisses that found them dancing in the waves and breathless in the sea. "I don't know what to say!" Cash finally managed.

"Don't say anything," Micah murmured, his hands caressing Cash's bare back. "I should… should have done this years ago."

"Me too!" Cash said, salt spray in his lips, Micah's lips on his lips, hands gripping his arms to stay upright in the surf. "I … I've wanted to for so long …"

Cash stumbled, gently, in the sand beneath his feet, right hand dipping beneath the waves. Only then did the reality of Micah's flawless, stunning nudity dawn on him. His fingers glanced across Micah's cock, thick and stiff in the frothy surf. He gasped, aloud, to finally touch that which had eluded him for so long.

Whatever grip he'd had on reality, on his self-control, on his previous life and all it had meant to him, disappeared in a moment. Forget the fact that he'd never been this far with a man before, had never wanted anything so badly in his life before, had never even touched another man this way before. Cash followed his instincts and, for once, let them guide him where they might.

Taking Micah's stiff prick in hand, he stroked it as gently as possible in the gently rolling sea. Micah murmured gratefully, mouth bending to gently kiss Cash's bare shoulder as Cash grabbed the small of his back with his left hand to steady himself. Thus buoyed, Cash gripped Micah more firmly, still tenderly, the water rushing back and away, revealing the glossy bronzed skin of his long, slender cock and the fat, mushroom tip, trembling and gleaming in the damp moonlight.

It was more beautiful than Cash had ever imagined: sleek and veiny, standing stiff and proud from his sparsely haired pubic thatch, tender and damp in his hand. He began to stroke harder, Micah murmuring and breathing atop his shoulder in reply.

"Jesus," he sputtered as Cash tended to him, eagerly lost in the moment and yet savoring every second of it. "I can't … it's coming … so … fast!" Micah exploded in Cash's hand, a dizzying blast of warm, wet silk in sharp contrast to the cool ocean current.

Cash gasped with delight, but no more so than when he continued to stroke Micah, milking him gently as his lover bit into his shoulder to keep from crying out once more as Cash's fingers gently caresses his trembling, shuddering skin.

Five

Micah clung to Cash, adrift in the sea, gasping with delight, Cash's salty flesh between his teeth as his former classmate milked him. He had never cum so quickly, so powerfully. Far from a virgin, he had merely grown overheated at the sight of Cash, drifting down toward the sea, long, tight, and hunky in a pair of baggies hanging from his lean, narrow hips.

When Cash had waded into the sea, eyes never leaving Micah's body, Micah knew then it would happen. Knew then that the boy he'd long admired, and fervently desired—all man now—felt the same way. It both shocked and thrilled him. Micah had always wondered about Cash. Was he? Wasn't he? The way he approached him, the way their eyes met and Cash sauntered into the sea, body lithe and limber and purposeful, he knew. Deep in his heart, he knew they felt the same way—about men, if not each other.

And, for the moment, that was enough for him.

Frozen in place even while his heart hammered with desire, Micah waited for the inevitable, then thrilled to Cash's gentle, tender kiss. He had never been kissed so tenderly before, so adoringly, as if Cash had imagined the moment a thousand times before and was cherishing the realization that it was finally happening.

Micah knew the feeling. As he and Cash drifted in the sea, hearts hammering against each other's chests, lips salty and slick with desire], Micah suddenly felt his nakedness turn to longing.

He hadn't even bothered sleeping, knowing he was too keyed up from the long bus ride, the trip to his father's gravesite, and, of course, the reunion with Cash.

When he'd drifted onto the back porch, the ocean called to him, and he'd answered willingly. Lingering on the shore with the beer from the fridge—he'd figured he'd replace it later—Micah had grown accustomed to the solitude. After a beer or two, it was as if he wasn't alone on the beach, but in the entire universe. Feeling frisky, he stripped off his shorts and T-shirt and stood naked in the surf. When no spotlights went off, sirens sounded, or cops showed up, he dove into the sea, emerging past the froth and standing in the quiet flatlands just beyond.

Cash's cottage looked quiet and peaceful, like his life, and in the silent stillness that surrounded him, Micah felt out of place. It was as if he'd spent the last few years running to stand still while his former classmate had put every single day to good use.

Cash was a man now, though his youthful face and lean, hard body still made him appear boyish and sexy as hell. But he had a life—a home, a business, roots—and a future. He didn't need Micah crashing on his couch for weeks, screwing up his life and sending his well-ordered routine on a detour he might not want to—and perhaps wasn't ready to—take.

Micah knew he didn't belong, and wouldn't stay. He'd already been planning his predawn escape when, lo and behold, Cash had emerged. Whatever escape Micah had been planning vanished with the smooth, easy smile that greeted him. He knew in that instant, as he knew now, he would stay long enough to play this out, for better or worse.

But first, he owed Cash an orgasm.

"Damn," he sputtered, licking the spray from Cash's shoulder and drifting left until their lips met and they kissed passionately in the surf. "I… I don't know what happened."

Cash's eyes were wide; he was panting. "I… I don't know, either. I… I've wanted to do that since the day I saw you."

"Then we're even," Micah murmured, taking his hand and dragging Cash from the surf. "Because I've *wanted* you to do that since the day I saw *you*."

They emerged from the sea, frothy and wet, Cash's baggies still dropping off his narrow hips. He'd been a swimmer in high school and even now kept his shape, a little fuller, perhaps, but in all the right places. Where he'd been bony and thin back in school, now his shoulders were broad, his arms muscular, chest chiseled and hairless. His marble pale skin glowed an alabaster white beneath the moon, and even more so with the seawater drifting down his lean, flat stomach into the waistband of his baggies.

They fell upon the sandy, rumpled towel Micah had snagged from the porch. "Micah, I..." Cash began, but he silenced him with a deep, breathless kiss.

"Not now," he said, urgently, the moon high above them, the crashing surf at their backs. Punctuating his demands with wet, feverish kisses, he lay Cash back on the towel and pressed his palms flat against his chest. "Give me this moment, Cash, and then we'll talk all you want, okay?"

Cash merely nodded, skin gleaming white beneath Micah's long, dark fingers.

"I can't tell you how many times I've fantasized about this," Micah murmured, dragging his hands down Cash's long, lean torso until they met the waistband of his baggies.

"Me too," Cash murmured, watching his every move.

"These are so big," Micah teased, tugging them gently. "I bet they'd slide right off your hips if I tugged just the slightest bit..."

Cash sat up. Or tried to, anyway. Micah put an end to that noise, with quickness. "Micah we can't! Not out here!"

He snorted in reply. "Cash, you just gave me a tug job in the ocean." He chuckled as Cash blushed at the term. "How is this any worse than that?"

Cash whimpered helplessly, just the way Micah liked him—flat on his back, aglow beneath the moonlight, dripping wet and squirming helplessly.

"I'll be quick," Micah promised, tugging all the more, until the baggies drifted down past his hips, revealing a glossy red bush. "Can *you* be quick, Cash?"

Cash nodded, biting his lower lip. "It's been so long, Micah, I can't believe I haven't cum already!"

"Not yet!" he teased, tugging the baggies down farther until at last his cock, fat and thick and hard, sprang into view. "You can't rob me of this after so damn long!"

Micah let the baggies drift to mid-knee, just enough to be out of his way, but enough to keep Cash's legs bound together should he try and bolt. He needn't have worried. Helplessly, happily, Cash squirmed and wriggled as Micah ran his fingers through his ginger bush.

"I knew you'd be red down here," he murmured, admiring the thick, unruly thatch and how vibrant and bold it looked against Cash's flat, hard belly. His fingers danced along the veiny shaft. "And this cock … I knew it would be thick."

He began to stroke it, watching Cash's eyes roll back in his head as his hands formed fists, bunching up the beach towel as he lay, splayed out for Micah's pleasure.

"So thick…" His voice was low and deep, admiring Cash's glistening cock as he stroked its pliant, supple skin. It was so soft and stiff, damp from the sea and also his desire, coating the thick, rigid staff with a drizzle of icing Micah yearned to lick, suck, and swallow.

But not tonight, he thought. Hands, tonight. And tomorrow? There would be time for mouths, lips, tongues, and so. Much. More. He hadn't given a good, old-fashioned hand job, just a handie, since God knows when. Suddenly, it was like they were back in school, all the years since graduation just fading away like the ocean waves as they fizzed into the shore at Cash's feet.

This could have been any summer night in Fiesta back then, hot and humid, the beach deserted, moon high above, two young lovers splayed out on a towel, one bent between the other's legs, his pants down, cock straining, wet and stiff in the other's hands.

Their eyes met, only briefly. Micah was too eager to worship his lover's cock to gaze adoringly into his eyes. His left hand fondled Cash's balls, full and thick, urging soft, panting sighs from his lips. Micah wanted to talk dirty, to encourage his lover, but he enjoyed listening to his moans and pants too much to drown them out with his own voice.

They began to come more quickly now, Cash's eyes squeezing shut, nipples hard amidst his rouged areolas, belly tightening, abs defined, thighs straining against his yanked down baggies, Micah tugging his balls with one hand, gently stroking him with the other when—he came, thrusting into Micah's wet, slippery grip before he shot his great, massive load all over his squirming chest.

He gasped, they both gasped, and Cash moaned in ecstasy, writhing as Micah milked him gently, tenderly, the way he'd milked him in the sea. A blush rose to Cash's cheeks, blistering under the milky white moonlight, green eyes wide as he peered up at Micah.

"Kiss me," was all he said.

Micah grinned. No one had ever asked him to do that before. "With pleasure," he murmured, falling atop Cash as they squirmed on top of the beach blanket, sandy and sticky with lust.

Six

The next day at lunch, Cash couldn't stop blushing. Everywhere he looked, people seemed to keep staring back at them. The back deck of Brioche, his favorite café, was full with a lively late lunch crowd. And yet each table, or so it seemed to Cash, was more concerned with what he and Micah were eating than what was on their own plates.

He felt as if everyone in town knew their secret, the secret he'd struggled so long to keep, even from Micah. Even from himself. Micah peered back at him from over his glass of sweet iced tea, wearing a curious expression.

"The hell is wrong with you?" He snorted before putting his glass back down on the crowded table.

Wanting Micah to have the full Brioche effect, Cash had taken the liberty of ordering nearly every appetizer on the menu. Now they sat, half eaten, in the midday sun.

Cash shrugged. The fact was, he didn't know what was wrong with him. "This just feels so funny," he explained, trying to put it into words. "Sitting here with you, out in public, plain as day…"

Suddenly, a cloud passed over Micah's beautiful face. "Don't tell me you're still in the closet," he said with a tone that indicated he clearly wasn't. They sat at a corner table, his favorite, though usually he sat there alone. He did most things alone. Not wanting to hurt another Susie Wannamaker in his life, too afraid to replace Micah with another man, he'd simply neutered himself, convincing himself that eating alone, going to movies alone, and being married to his job was any kind of life.

Now he leaned closer to Micah, images of what they'd done earlier that morning on the beach flashing through his mind. "I'm not in or out of anything," he insisted, keeping his voice low just the same. "I'm just…me."

Micah leaned back, crossed his arms over an old Sweet Tooth T-shirt Cash had loaned him and smirked knowingly. "So what if I was to reach my hand across the table and put it on yours right now? What would that do to you?"

Cash almost flinched at the suggestion, giving Micah the answer he was looking for.

"You know what year it is right?" he teased, making Cash blush all over again—this time for a very different reason.

"Yes, and you know how small this town is, Micah. How judgmental it is. How intolerant it can be."

Micah waved a dismissive hand. "That's a copout, man, and you know it."

Cash nodded. "Maybe it is, but what kept you from telling me how you felt back in high school, huh? It's not like I'm the only one who kept a secret all those years, Micah."

They peered at one another across the crowded table, and Micah finally nodded. "That was years ago, Cash. How long are you going to live a lie?"

"It's not a lie exactly, just more a sin of omission."

Micah smirked. "You know, it might've felt like one at the time, but what we did last night wasn't a sin, Cash." Just then the waitress came, making Cash sit up abruptly, as if they'd been caught. Micah watched him while the waitress bundled up the food and took it back to the kitchen to put in to go boxes.

"Is this how it's going to be? You jumping every time a waitress comes around? Looking over your shoulder every time we're close?"

Cash wanted more than anything to reach across the table, take Micah's hand, and smother it with soft, velvet kisses. "Not all the time, just … let me adjust to 'Hurricane Micah' first, okay?"

They both laughed, but Cash was only half joking. He meant what he said. Like a hurricane, Micah had swept into Cash's life well-ordered life and threatened to blow it—and him—away completely. "I've built a life here, a good life—"

"A perfect life, is more like it!" Micah huffed.

Cash shook his head, struggling to find the words. "It's far from perfect, but it's… it's…"

"Safe?" Micah offered.

Cash nodded, almost defensively. "It's not a sin to play it safe, you know."

Micah paused, as if considering Cash's words. His expression softened and he slid his hand across the table to just shy of Cash's. "I'm not here to judge you, Cash. I'm not here to mess up a good thing, either. I just thought, while I'm here, I might try and make it a little better for a while. You know? Is that so wrong?"

Cash sagged with relief to hear Micah's tender words. "You already have," he insisted. He gently brushed Cash's fingertips just as the waitress appeared. They both stiffened, then laughed aloud at their abrupt reaction. The waitress, young enough to still be in high school, wrinkled her nose as if they were already old men.

"Would either of you gentlemen care for dessert?"

They snickered once more, before Cash nodded and said, "A slice of Key lime pie and two forks, please."

"And two cups of coffee," Micah said to her back as she turned to return to the kitchen.

"Speaking of while you're here, how long do you plan on staying?" Cash tried and failed to hide the naked desperation in his trembling voice.

Micah seemed to sense it, brushing it off with his usual good humor. "Why, you ready to put a ring on it after one night together?"

They laughed some more, a rare and bubbly sound in Cash's life. Blushing anew, Cash shrugged. "No, I'm just saying…do you have any idea of how long you might be in town?"

Micah looked past the weathered fence bordering the bistro's back deck. His eyes held a faraway look until they peered back at Cash. "I have enough money to stick around for a few days…"

"You don't need money, Micah. You can stay at my place for free."

Micah stiffened slightly. "I like to pay my own way."

Cash gave him a playful grin. "Where you always this stubborn back in school?"

Micah's sudden burst of laughter alarmed the last few tables straggling after lunch. "Where you always this *bossy*?" he teased back.

They were still laughing when the waitress appeared, clearing the last of the plates before sliding down two coffees, a cream and sugar service, and the biggest slice of Key lime pie north of Miami. Before they could fight about the bill, and eager for a little more privacy, Cash handed her a hundred dollar bill and told her to keep the change.

Reaching for a spoon, Micah arched one eyebrow before winking. "I've never been a kept man before; I kind of like it." They ate in silence for a few stolen minutes, savoring the rich Key lime pie while chasing it with warm, strong coffee.

The day stretched out before them, long and lazy, and Cash's brain felt fuzzy after their sleepless night together. With his float day at work, he had nothing to do but savor every moment with his late night lover. But he wanted more than that. He knew it was too soon to expect any kind of commitment, especially when they knew so little about each other, but the way Micah made it sound, he was ready to cut bait and run in the next forty-eight hours.

"Speaking of being a kept man, I was wondering…"

Micah paused, the last bite of Key lime pie on the way to his luscious, full lips. "I'm listening."

Cash grinned. "I was just thinking, and there's no easy way to say this to a contemporary, but I was hoping maybe, if it's not too offensive…"

Micah rolled his eyes. "Jesus, man, just spit it out already!"

Cash chuckled. "Come work for me."

When Micah's eyes widened at the suggestion, Cash insisted, "You said spit it out."

Micah nodded, finishing off the pie and washing it down with dark, rich coffee. "What?" he asked doubtfully. "You mean like selling jellybeans to school kids or something? You know I've got a job waiting on me in South Beach, right?"

Cash waved a hand reassuringly, despite the disappointment he felt every time Micah reminded him how short their sexy reunion would be. "If you're half as good as I think you are, Micah, this job won't take you that long. And then … then you'll be free to go wherever you like."

Micah smirked. "So it's *not* selling jelly beans then?"

Cash chuckled and nodded toward the naked brick wall across the alley from where they sat. He hadn't just chosen the secluded seat in the corner of Brioche's back deck for more privacy. Long before deciding where to eat lunch, he'd had ulterior motives. They both looked at the long, wide, bland wall. It stretched the length of the Sweet Tooth, a long swath of exposed brick Cash had been meaning to do something with ever since he bought the place.

But something had always come up to distract him from the project. A new walk-in cooler, patching on the roof, or the brand-new display cases he'd ordered earlier that year. But now he had the perfect idea two kill two birds with one beautiful, talented stone. That is, if Micah agreed to do it.

"What about it?" Micah asked.

Cash raised his hands in a viewfinder position like some A-list Hollywood director. "I've been meaning to hire someone to cover that wall with a mural. Something fun and colorful to accent the store. I thought with your particular skill set, and you being in need of a little spending money, you might paint one for me?"

Micah studied the wall carefully for moment, his face neutral, before turning back to Cash. He winked and, just like that, Cash knew he was in.

"What kind of spending money are we talking here?" he teased. When Cash went to answer, Micah held up a hand almost defensively. "I'm just kidding. Of course I'll do it. On one condition."

Cash pretended to consider the option, as if he could refuse Micah anything. "Which is…?"

He shrugged, like it was no big thing. "Just complete and utter creative control, that's all."

Cash grinned, sitting back; mission accomplished. Pinning Micah with grateful eyes he said, "I would expect nothing less from an artiste of your caliber, Micah."

Micah screwed up his face, wagging a warning finger. "How do you know I'm any good anyway, Cash? I'm just some guy you went to school with, you know."

Cash felt the blush rise to his cheeks, looking away before glancing back at his midnight lover. "I didn't just recognize your dad from one art show, Micah," he confessed. "I used to go every year."

"Why?" Micah wondered aloud.

"To see your latest paintings, dummy!" Cash grunted, downplaying his fascination with Micah's artwork and not wanting him to know how much it meant to him—then and now.

"So, complete creative control, huh?" Micah grinned. "Be careful what you wish for, my friend. Be careful what you wish for…"

Seven

Micah skated through downtown Fiesta, a bright, sunny shopping district lined with surf shops, souvenir stands, shell shops, and more than its share of taco stands and shaved ice booths.

It was mid afternoon, his belly full and spirits bright as he swerved around parking meters and the rare pedestrian on the way to his old haunt, the Art Mart.

Although they'd planned to spend the rest of the day together, Cash had gotten a frantic text just after dessert. Something about a missing box of Red Vines a regular customer was looking for. Begging off another slice of Key lime pie, Cash had walked promptly across the alley and into the store; *his* store. When he hadn't returned some twenty minutes later, Micah grew tired of staring at the plain brick wall and decided to do something about it.

Grabbing his trusty long board, he had skated across Ocean Drive and now, ten minutes later, was in front of Fiesta's only arts and crafts store. During high school, Micah had spent every spare minute—not to mention spare dime—at the Art Mart, stocking up on his favorite sketchpads and charcoal pens.

Back then the place had seemed giant to him, a wonderland of endless aisles, each more colorful than the next, filled with rows and rows of rubber stamps and model paints and swatches of felt in every hue of the rainbow. A kindly old woman named Edna had always asked to see what he was drawing. In all those years, he'd never had the balls to show her.

Now it seemed too late. A college kid, only a year or two younger than Micah himself, manned the counter. He had dyed black hair, foppish and combed over to one side like a wave breaking over his right ear. Painful looking tribal ear piercings, a nose ring, and the obligatory skull tattoo above his shirt collar completed the rebellious look.

He gave Micah a cursory glance before returning to the sales flier by the cash register. Micah felt like a prehistoric mosquito trapped in amber as he walked straight to the aisle where the sketchpads where kept. His funds were running low until Cash paid him a deposit on the mural, so Micah grabbed just one pad and two charcoal pens. Even that would strain his paltry budget, but he couldn't imagine spending his money on anything else.

"Where's Edna?" Micah asked as the kid rang up his order.

His face bordering on a sneer, the kid grunted, "Who?"

"Never mind," Micah grunted back. He pocketed his change and headed out the door. As if on autopilot, Micah did as he always did after a fresh Art Mart score. Sliding a charcoal pen in each pocket, he tucked the pad under his left arm, hopped on his board, and headed straight toward Shady Palms Park.

It was a rundown park on the rough side of town—shabby, grungy, and rarely used. That's what Micah liked about it. He often had the place to himself, a little oasis tucked away, two blocks from the beach and bordering a small lake lined with clustered palms and half a dozen benches.

Times had changed, however, and now suburbia had encroached on his scruffy little park. Two new subdivisions had sprung up where a vacant lot and a ragged strip mall had once stood. The sidewalks were smooth beneath his rolling skateboard and the park had gotten a facelift, too. The jungle gym had been painted, the swings repaired, and fresh mulch lain along the walking paths.

It was still quiet for this time of day, the sun just right as he chose his favorite bench along the soft, rippling lake. Children's voices roamed playfully on the breeze, the occasional giggle and shout reaching him as he settled in. It felt strange to be sitting there again. It all felt strange, every minute he'd spent in Fiesta.

From the minute the bus had dropped him off on the outskirts of town, he had felt like a stranger and, yet, oddly familiar. Perhaps it was the rootless nature of this new journey. When he'd left Fiesta after high school, he had a destination in mind. A place to go, even if he was a semester early. Leaving Atlanta this time, he left only a generic dorm room behind. He had nothing to hold him back and nowhere to invite him in.

He had only the money in his pocket, the clothes on his back, and his wits. He was not without skills or, for that matter, experience. Halfway to his art degree, he had interned like the rest of his classmates at every sort of ad agency and marketing company, and even spent one hot Georgia summer as a house painter.

Any of those still skills would stand him in good stead on the open job market. But it felt odd being a man without a country. Seeing Cash, more than walking into his father's sterile apartment, had felt like home. A safe place to land, and a warm spot to rest his weary bones. And yet, the more he saw of Cash's carefully calculated and well-manicured life, the less he wanted to intrude.

Suddenly, the mural seemed both a fitting tribute to their time together as well as a simple way to repay Cash his kindness for taking him in. He'd done a similar size mural for a class project his sophomore year, and from planning to completion it had taken less than a week. That might be just enough time to make Cash his secret lover, pay his debt, put a little money in his pocket, and leave something of himself behind when he inevitably stole away before daybreak after it was through.

As much as he cared for Cash, Micah had no interest in skulking around Fiesta resisting the urge to hold his lover's hand or kiss his cheek in public. He'd heard what his friends had called the outsiders back in school, even those Micah knew were straight: fag, queer, cocksucker... and worse. He knew how closely the cool kids watched anyone who wasn't one of them, hoping for the slightest sign of difference, the slightest hint of being other than them. Going away to school had freed him from Fiesta's small town conservatism, but being back made his shoulders tense all over again.

He was far from an activist, but if his father's rebuke had taught him anything it was simply this: if your own flesh and blood couldn't even love you for who you were, then no stranger ever would. His fellow students back in high school, the PE coaches with their off color remarks, the librarians who arched an eyebrow if you asked for anything other than *Sports Illustrated* or car magazines, they would never be more than curious, and never be anything less than suspicious.

So why spend time living for someone else, or by their rules?

On his own since the age of eighteen, Micah had made his own rules and they'd worked well enough—until now. Clearly, Cash had his own set of rules as well. Rules that kept him locked in time, trapped in a world that barely let him breathe, let alone love. Sexy as he was, Micah didn't want to enjoy Cash just in the shadows.

If he and Cash weren't free to express whatever they felt for each other, whenever they wanted to, then they might as well be back in high school pining away for each other from afar. He'd rather move forward than backward, even if it meant being alone. And if it meant losing Cash, at least he'd have had him at all.

Whatever happened now, however long he stayed or however soon he left, Micah would always have that first tender, adoring kiss in the sea, proving for once that fantasies really *do* come true.

But unlike fairytales, not all fantasies had a happy ending and the fact that Cash had chosen to spend his life in the closet so far was proof enough that he'd never be Micah's Prince Charming— even if they *were* perfect together. Maybe he'd come out one day, or maybe he wouldn't. Could Micah afford to wait? Could he be the man who would one day drag Cash out of the closet, even if it *was* kicking and screaming?

Micah shoved away the thought, eager to come up with something special to show his friend his appreciation, commitment, and loyalty after all these years. He flipped open the sketchpad to the very first page, grabbing a pen and holding it aloft.

Visualizing the long black brick wall, he sketched a rough proximity and got to work. Time passed and the breeze gently rustled the quietly filling pages of his new sketchpad. False starts and botched ideas made quick work of the first dozen pages. Not wanting to burn through the entire pad on his first day, Mica lay it down on the bench beside him to rest his eyes. He'd been lost in thought for so long, and now the sights and sounds of his surroundings slowly came into focus.

Behind him, two mothers—one white, the other black—were just wrapping up a play date with their kids in the park. *Progress,* he thought to himself, not sure if he was being ironic or legit. They had been mere background noise while he sketched, burning through ideas that didn't pan out, struggling for inspiration. But now, eyes, fingers, and brain strained from the effort, he watched them come a little closer.

They were merry little children, aged four, five, or six, he couldn't tell. He'd never been good with ages, and little kids always seemed so foreign to him. Tiny faces flush from the monkey bars, little butts sandy from the slide, they giggled and shouted as they approached the park's entrance.

"Hold hands," one of the mothers said as they paused to cross the street. Without hesitation, they reached out for the hand nearest to them. A little black boy held hands with a little white girl, two brown girls reached out and clasped each other's fingers, while two boys, lingering in the back, did the same.

Without hesitation, without shame or doubt, the little black boy reached for the little white boy's hand and laced their fingers automatically. Micah had rarely seen anything so innocent and beautiful at the same time. The light changed, they crossed the street, and the minute they were on the opposite sidewalk, fingers and hands drifted apart to punch, tug, and horseplay once more.

It seemed even more fitting that way, that what should be so monumental for Micah was but another day in the park for six innocent children. Suddenly inspired, he picked up his pad and his pen, flipped to a new page, and began sketching as if his life depended on it.

Eight

Cash didn't realize he was all aglow until Gus Connors, the old salt who ran the Flamingo Diner across from the Sweet Tooth, moved the perpetual toothpick wedged between his thin lips to one side and winked.

"Who's the lucky lady, Cash?"

Cash blinked, as if being yanked back to reality from a particularly sweet daydream. "Huh? What?" he murmured, the two words running together like some over the top reaction in a rom-com.

Gus nodded toward the two jumbo size Styrofoam cups full of homemade lemonade he'd just poured while the cook made the rest of Cash's lunch order. "How long we known each other, boy?"

Gus was an old salt, his wiry arms covered with tattoos from a short stint in the Navy, apron greasy, T-shirt greasier, smile constantly leering at one of the young, pretty waitresses that ran around his busy restaurant, day and night, in their tight pink "Flamingo Diner" aprons.

But he made great patty melts, and even better French fries, and was right across the street from his store, after all—making Cash a frequent and loyal customer.

"Couple of years," Cash said hesitantly, thinking that's more than Gus had ever said to him in all that time. "W-w-why?"

Gus leered like maybe they were ready to go out hunting together—hunting humans, that is. "And in all that time, I've never seen you order lunch for two before."

The heat that rose to Cash's face could have rivaled the spitfire grill in Gus's greasy kitchen for sure. "Oh, well, I mean…" he stammered, looking out the plate glass window across the street toward where Micah stood on a ladder, wearing a pair of Cash's cargo pants that had started sliding down his waist—and no shirt.

"I hired an old friend of mine to paint a mural on the side of the store and I figure I should feed him, right?"

Gus followed Cash's gaze toward Micah, his long, bronze body gleaming in the sun, biceps flexing as he sealed the bricks before applying his first coat of paint. He could have been modeling something—ladders, maybe? Baggy cargo pants? Paintbrushes?— if only there'd been a camera crew around to document it instead of just Cash's admiring, adoring eyes.

Today? Cash thought to himself, desire tightening his throat as he found it hard to draw his eyes away from Micah's lean, flawless body as it glistened in the sun. *Today of all days he had to work on the mural topless?*

Cash remembered where he was and turned back to find Gus giving him a cold, hard stare. Gone was the casual humor of "guy talk" when he thought he'd been bringing lunch to some mystery girl.

Now Gus's voice was as lean and cold as his stare. "Seen him around here a lot lately, Cash," he said, the tone of accusation heavy on his tongue, the look of scorn dark and foreboding in his eyes.

Cash shrugged, trying to keep his voice even and hoping he was just overreacting. "Like I said, Gus, we're old classmates and haven't seen each other in years."

Gus continued to study him carefully. So carefully Cash began to wilt under the intense gaze, armpits and forehead growing damp with sweat. "Looks like you're making up for lost time now, huh?"

Cash cocked his head. "I don't... I mean..."

Gus waved an old dishrag, the one he often used to endlessly clean the counter beside his cash register. "Seen you two gallivanting around all morning together," he said, obviously referring to the planning session Micah had insisted on, teasing him playfully the whole time about how he should charge him by the brick.

Cash tried to picture how it might look to Gus, peering out from his diner windows. With only the two lanes of Ocean Drive between them, he might as well have been watching a giant movie screen in his living room. He turned back from admiring Micah to find Gus, leathery lips frowning, limp blue eyes narrowing.

"Just exactly what kind of friends were you two back in school, anyway?" he wondered aloud, clearly having cooked up an answer for himself.

Cash froze, unsure how to respond. He could have huffed and bluffed, or begged and borrowed, but he felt frozen in place. All the fears he'd had about him and Micah setting local tongues wagging had suddenly come true, seemingly overnight.

He'd spent years hiding his secret, making sure not to let his eyes linger on handsome young customers too long, making a big deal over whatever hot young girl came in the store, keeping up appearances, playing it straight, only to see it all unravel Micah's first week in town.

And they'd barely even done anything! When Cash had suggested the mural to Micah, he hadn't realized it would consume his live-in lover. Between plotting and planning, sketching and scratching, sweating and straining—and not in a good way— they'd barely seen each other. Cash was too chicken to ask Micah to sleep in his room with him, where something might have happened, and even if he had, Micah was such a workaholic he could barely sit still before leaping up and grabbing his sketchpad to scribble down a new inspiration.

It was like being married, without the sex!

A bell rang behind Gus just then, and two Styrofoam boxes appeared in the steamy kitchen window. Cash nearly sagged with relief. He'd been coming into the Flamingo Diner on the regular since he opened the Sweet Tooth, and had never heard this particular tone from Gus before. It was sudden, shocking, and cold, leaving Cash feeling vulnerable and unsure, like someone had just ripped the black and white tiled diner floor right out from under him.

Sliding the to-go containers from the window, Gus opened them each, whistling at the contents as if they were evidence of some heinous crime Cash was about to commit.

"You won't catch me serving the help lunch," he said, closing the lids with a grunt before shoving both boxes in a plastic bag. "Let alone the deluxe patty melt special, that's for damn sure."

Cash tried to shrug it off. "You know what they say," he chattered inanely, mind reeling and voice sounding very, very small. "A full worker is a happy worker."

Gus shoved the bag across the counter, just not quite far enough for Cash to take it yet. "A happy worker's one thing, Cash," he said in that same accusatory tone. "But the way you look at that there boy, ordering him the jumbo lemonade and deluxe lunch special, well… makes me think he's working on more than just your paint job, know what I mean?"

The world fell away just then. Gus's eyes, cold and probing, bored into his own. Cash had a twenty held out for the order and, peeling his eyes away, threw it on the counter. He grabbed the bag and slid it over his wrist before reaching for his two to-go cups. But Gus wasn't through with him yet. Grabbing his wrist, he held it in a vise-like grip. "Why, if I didn't know better, son," he said, just shy of a growl. "I'd think you two had taken up together…"

Cash gasped. "W-w-what?" he stammered, backing away and yanking his arm free in the process. He'd gripped the cup too tightly, popping the lid and sending lemonade gushing all over Gus's precious counter. He dropped the cup altogether, watching it roll onto the floor, spilling ice in every direction as he backed toward the door. "I… I …"

His voice was drowned out by the cowbell clanging overhead as he backed through the door, a wave of lemonade following him from the spilled cup. He turned, gasping for breath as the door shut behind him, wondering what the hell he'd done—and what might happen next.

Nine

Micah stepped from the ladder at last, stretching his sore, aching back and turning off the construction lights he'd picked up at the hardware store around the corner on Sandpiper Street. He stretched some more in the darkness of the alley between the Sweet Tooth and Brioche Café, the dim light soothing after his long, hot day.

The scaffolding he'd ordered from Home Emporium had been delivered a few hours earlier but he'd been too tired to put them all together. Now he sat heavily on the stack of paint splattered plywood and rested his weary legs.

Micah was gym strong, but it had been a while since he'd worked a full day, let alone one in the sweltering Florida sun. He'd been grateful when it had finally set a few hours earlier, and even more so now as he reached for his shirt, the damp sweat finally beginning to dry in the cool ocean breeze.

Fortunately Cash had brought him the biggest patty melt and Styrofoam container of lemonade he'd ever seen, which had lasted him all day. If only he'd stuck around long enough to share it with him. Or hell, even watch him eat it.

Instead Cash had handed them to him, mumbled something about "doing inventory," and hustled back into the candy store without so much as a backward glance, to say nothing of blowing his newest employee a kiss.

Okay, sure, Micah hadn't expected a sweltering make out session or tug job in full view of half the town of Fiesta, but … would a smile have killed him? A wink?

That had been hours ago and, now, his body sore from the long work day, skin sticky with sweat and sun, Micah wanted nothing more than to scrub himself up in the employee bathroom and spend a quiet evening with Cash on his back deck overlooking the ocean.

He stood, inspired by the thought, and peered once more out across the downtown shopping district. He'd forgotten how small and sleepy Fiesta could be, rolling up the sidewalks promptly at nine every night. Now, at nearly eleven, the entire town felt like the beach had that first night with Cash: quiet, serene, deserted, almost … apocalyptic.

If only it felt like home.

He turned and, the work spotlights cool enough now to move, brought them into the back stock room for safekeeping overnight. Cash had propped the door open for him earlier that day so he could pop in from time to time and cool off, grab a bottle of water, or take a piss. Now he slid the lamps just inside the door—he'd have to work night and day if he wanted to finish in a week—and locked it tight behind him.

The store was silent, having closed an hour earlier, and he didn't see Cash anywhere. Dipping into the bathroom, Micah scrubbed up as best he could, washing off his chest and damp armpits, the front and back of his neck, and dousing his face before drying up with a handful of paper towels.

Feeling slightly more refreshed, he slipped into the break room for a bottle of water—finding a few hidden beers instead. Smirking to himself, as if he was getting away with something, Micah grabbed one. Then, on impulse, grabbed one more.

Taking a long, slow swig before leaving the break room, he approached the swinging half-door between the back and the front of the store only to find Cash leaning against the sales counter. There was a legal pad beside him, lines and checks and columns scribbled on the top page, a pencil lying across it casually. The store was closed, the lights all off save for the glow of the display cases, one on either side of the cash register.

His apron was off, his soft green shirt with crisp white lettering spelling out "Sweet Tooth" tight on his lean torso. Cash hadn't seen him yet, so Micah watched him from behind the display cases loaded with jelly beans and red vines, chocolates and lollipops.

Normally upbeat to a fault, Micah had never seen Cash wear such a pensive, stoic expression before. His green eyes looked softer than usual, sadder, too, almost … hurt. Micah could have stood and admired him from afar all day, but the pained expression made the friend—and lover—in him take a step closer instead. He pressed against the swinging door, making it squeak—and Cash jump.

"Shit!" he gasped, hand literally leaping to his chest as if they were sitting in a theater watching a horror movie. "I forgot you were here!"

Micah frowned. "Is that the thanks I get for sweating my ass off sketching out your mural all day?" he teased. "*And* bringing you a beer?"

The blush rose easily to Cash's expressive face. "I just meant… thank you." He took the beer as Micah inched close enough to offer it. "You done for the day?"

Micah nodded, leaning back against the counter across from him as the heat and work and tension drained from his body. "You?"

Cash peered down at the inventory list, then nodded. "My heart's just not in it tonight, you know?"

Micah nodded. His body and mind were settled, worn from the wearying day but also at peace. He was safe here, safe with Cash, safe in this moment, and wanted Cash to feel safe as well.

"What's wrong?" he asked, sliding his foot forward until the toes of their sneakers touched. "You've been distant ever since you brought me lunch." He pretended to fish in his pocket for some money. "You're mad I didn't go Dutch, right?"

Cash grinned bashfully, as if not used to being teased. "It's not that," he said, their eyes meeting in the small space behind the counter. "I just … some people will never be happy, you know?"

Micah sensed the tone in his voice, hopeless and futile. "What people?" he asked.

Cash shrugged. "I mean, I've worked hard to build a life here and give it meaning, you know? Worked hard to be a part of this community, give back to the community, and at the first sign of trouble, of imperfection…"

His voice cracked, a tender sound that made Micah want to help. "Who hurt you, Cash? What happened today?"

Their eyes met and, after a moment, he smiled. "Nothing I can't handle, Micah," he said, grinning wider. "Now that you're here."

Micah felt a spike in his heartbeat, a surge in his bloodstream. No one had ever made him feel so welcome before, not like Cash had. Suddenly, his blood wasn't the only thing surging. "Listen," he said, before downing the last of his beer. "I've been out in that hot sun all day, working up quite a sweat—"

"I know," Cash interrupted, waving his beer. "I feel so bad, you out there in that hot sun all day…"

Micah waved his hand. "That's not what I meant, Cash. I meant … I was working up a sweat, thinking about you."

He seemed surprised. "Really?"

Micah nodded, inching closer, just as they had that night in the ocean. "Why?" he teased. "You haven't been thinking about me?"

Cash grinned, his blush giving him away. "Only every spare minute."

"Oh yeah? What were you thinking about?"

Micah didn't think it was possible, but Cash blushed even more. "I was thinking, how… how your sweat might taste."

Micah grinned, toe to toe with his redheaded lover. "Is that right? And now? You still want a taste of your hot, sweaty employee?"

"Here?" Cash asked, peering over his shoulder at the storefront windows.

Micah shrugged, running his hand along Cash's lean, flat belly. "No one's around this late," he murmured, hand dipping lower to tease the button of his cargo pants. "And even if they were, Cash, we're behind this big old counter here…"

Micah's right hand slid along the front panel of Cash's pants, finding him already stiff and hard, while his left hand tugged his shorts gently down. Pants sliding around his narrow hips, Cash pushed him away playfully. "You said I could taste *your* sweat, remember?"

Micah gasped at the sudden show of affection, tumbling back against the display case behind him. "I did at that," he murmured breathlessly as Cash greedily tugged at his tank top. "I did at that."

Cash made quick work of the shirt and, true to his word, pressed full, greedy lips against his damp, sticky chest. He kissed and licked at Micah's bare flesh, hands tugging desperately at his belt, button, and zipper.

In no time Micah's pants were around his ankles, his boxers quick to follow as Cash sank to his knees and crouched, ass on his feet, pressing his full lips against Micah's belly, trembling anew.

"Cash, I…" he murmured, hands drifting to Cash's shoulders. "I didn't expect…"

Cash looked up, smiling. "I've been wanting this all day," he said breathlessly, right hand stroking Micah's thigh on the way up to his stiff, straining cock. "Please, just … let me lick every inch of sweat off you."

Micah gushed at the thought, cock leaping into Cash's hands as his lover stroked him gently, moistly in the dim display counter lighting. "Well, I've got about seven and a half inches you can start off with if you're *really* thirsty!"

They laughed, the sound rich and husky, but Cash was deadly serious. He inhaled Micah, body and soul, licking and kissing and sucking his skin as his hungry lips traveled his pelvis to the base of his stiff, raging prick. His lips drifted across Micah's pubic thatch, thick and redolent and damp, before his tongue glanced out to lick the base, then up the long, shuddering side.

Micah was fully erect now and drizzling with desire as Cash licked every throbbing vein and pulsing wrinkle along the way to the thick, throbbing tip. He was tender and gentle and slow, achingly slow, so that by the time his lips writhed along the leaking tip Micah gasped and moaned.

Cash's lips clung tightly to his rod, in a way no other man's had before. This was not a duty to perform or a chore to endure, but a moment to savor and enjoy. At least, that's how Cash made it feel. He seemed to relish every inch, lips slick and wet and tongue gripping the underside of Micah's straining prick as it rasped along his veiny skin.

As the tender liquor from their dual desire began to drizzle and slide from Cash's mouth, he caught it with his hand, stroking the daring inches of Micah's cock his lips couldn't—or wouldn't—reach. The sensation was sudden and slick and seismic, making the normally resilient Micah putty in his lover's thick, swollen mouth.

"Jesus," he gasped as Cash licked and sucked and stroked, undeterred. "I … I…"

Cash got the hint and slid his lips off and to one side, playing Micah's slick cock like a harmonica as he came in great, bursting gushes onto the floor. Micah had never come that fast before, nor that much, and when the torrent finally drizzled to a trickle, Cash brazenly slid his lips back around and encased the tip once more in his hot, tender mouth, sucking him dry in more ways than one.

Tender and sensitive, Micah chuckled and gently pressed his lover away from his crotch. "Damn," he murmured, sliding down to kiss and compliment him. "That was some kind of sexy."

Cash grinned, almost bashfully, particularly considering where those wet, glossy lips had just been a moment earlier. "Really?" he asked. "I … I've never done that before."

"Bullshit!"

Cash shook his head. "I never," he began, breathlessly. "I just never had the chance before."

Micah shook his head, correcting him. "You just never *took* the chance before."

Cash nodded. "I suppose so…"

Micah kissed him then, sad to think his friend had been living half a life out of fear. "Maybe … maybe that's why I showed up," he said. "Maybe I'm here right now to remind you to take a chance now and then."

He laughed. "Or maybe you were just supposed to be my first at all of… this."

Micah nodded. "So … you've never given head before but, tell me you've at least *gotten* some from a guy before, right?"

Cash bit his lip and shook his head. "Oh hell no," Micah said, shoving him back against the counter. "We're going to change that right here and now."

Ten

Cash stood on trembling legs, heart pounding, face flushed, his head awhirl. Ever since the run-in with Gus, he'd been somber, morose, quietly panicking for the old, safe life he'd led and the new, frightening one that might lie in wait.

Avoiding Micah like the plague, he'd tried to focus on inventory, only to find himself staring off into the distance, either blushing with shame or fuming with anger. As if going through all the stages of grief in one afternoon, he'd been sad, mad, disbelieving, disgusted, disappointed, and, ultimately, numb.

Between Gus's harsh words and the river of lemonade, he knew he could never go back to the Flamingo Diner. Just as well; he never wanted to. But still, crusty as he was, Gus was the town crier.

Everyone who was anyone in Fiesta, Florida stopped by the Flamingo Diner before the week was out, either to sample one of Gus's homemade pies or his pot luck stew or simply sit and chew the fat. And oh, what fat there'd be to chew once Gus started jawing about the scene Cash had made that day, to say nothing of the sexy young stud he'd hired to paint his building.

For hours Cash had pictured the slow demise of his business, his life, his future, and for another few hours he'd realized he didn't quite care. If Gus—a man he'd known for years—could turn on him in an instant, who else might be lurking in the shadows, sharpening their knives as well?

And then, as if in answer to his prayer, Micah appeared, sweaty and sultry, damp and dewy and bearing, of all things, a fresh, cold beer. He'd sipped it eagerly, when all he wanted was his lover's damp cock, wet and buried deep in his mouth.

There, he'd said it! If only to himself. Cash was suddenly certain of only one thing: he wanted Micah, as much of him as he could have, for as long as he could have, and he didn't care who knew it.

As if sensing his inner turmoil, Micah had offered the best remedy: himself. Okay, *and* his cock! Long and gleaming, musky and fragrant and meaty and firm, it had been all Cash had ever imagined, and more. And to lick the thick, clotted icing from the tip after he'd come had been a most savory and unexpected treat, a rare moment in his life where the reality had topped the fantasy.

And it wasn't over; not even close. "Micah," he murmured, back pressed against the counter as he tugged off his shirt. "You don't have to do this…"

"Have to?" Micah scoffed, dragging his pants down as he fondled him with a damp, sticky hand. "I want to, Cash. I've been wanting to since that night on the beach." Micah's voice was warm against his cheek before he dragged full, wet lips against Cash's own. "I just want to take this slow, you know?"

Cash nodded, lips crashing against his lover's. "I know," he gasped when their mouths finally parted. "I want…"

Micah squeezed his cock, stiff and sticky with eagerness. "I know what you want, Cash. Now shut up and let me give it to you."

Before he did, Micah kissed him again, soft and lovely, long and meaningful, a lover's kiss—it had to be. Drifting from Cash's lips, Micah kissed his jaw line, his chin, his neck, each shoulder, and each hard, peaked nipple—all while tenderly stroking his manhood to an aching, throbbing stiffness.

At last he crouched, bare ass pressing against the back of his feet, knees jutting out, hands sliding to his hips as he began to pepper the tip of Cash's cock with wet, feverish kisses. He slid his tongue along the damp and dewy tip, collecting a pearl of pre-cum and slathering it all around the glossy head.

Cash had promised himself he'd be strong, he'd last, he'd remain silent and stoic, but all that flew out the window the minute Micah's lips enrobed the tip of his trembling cock in their volcanic heat. He whimpered and cooed, he wriggled his hips and thrust his ass, he cried out and shook and Micah gently calmed him with sweet, sucking, succulent strokes of his lips and tongue.

He took it slow, agonizingly slow, until Cash found his rhythm and, clinging to the counter behind him, a hand on either side of his writhing hips, fingers tense and knuckles white, he gave himself to the moment.

Micah's fingers were long and smooth along his hips, gripping him tightly as he bobbed his head in a slow, gentle rhythm. His lips clung tightly, then parted slightly to vaguely hover and slide along the glossy, pliant skin of his prick.

Micah's tongue swirled and danced along the tip, joining his lips in a perfect storm of sweet, swollen affection. Despite his gentle sucking and tender licking, his patience and persistence, soon enough Cash was at his breaking point, desire bubbling over.

The soft, molten heat of Micah's mouth, the slightest glance of his lips, the tight rasping of his tongue, the newness of the experience, and his own eager excitement found him powerless to resist. "Micah, I…" he panted. "I … I'm…"

Micah slid his lips away with an agonizing drag along his swollen, surging cock until they glanced across the tip just before it erupted in a throbbing blast of pure, wet lust. Nearly five years of pent-up desire and late-night fantasies throbbed and spit from the swollen tip, joining Micah's clotted desire on the tiled floor.

Micah waited out the fiercest bursts, stroking and milking him gently as Cash shivered and spat. When the first wave had passed he slid his lips back around the tip to savor the last fine drops, making Cash cry out in delight and, gently, sag to the floor.

They sat, face to face after that, safely hidden behind the display cases, the soft white light flattering Micah's dark, damp skin. Naked save for the pair of sticky briefs dangling around one ankle, Cash sat shamelessly, openly, across from his lover.

Their skin was slick with sweat, lips puffy from kissing—and more. Micah shook his head, smirking playfully. "You've honestly never done that before?" he asked.

Cash shook his head. "Would I lie about something that pitiful?"

Micah scolded him with his eyes. "It's not pitiful, exactly," he teased. "It's kind of… sexy. Sharing that with you, I mean. For the first time."

"Think of how it felt for me, Micah. Sharing it with you."

"What do you mean?"

Cash shrugged, figuring it was too late to turn back now. "Every time I thought about… that… I thought about doing it with you. I'm not sure any other guy could have measured up the first time, and I'm glad, now, I'll never have to find out."

Micah reached for his hand across the floor and, together, they sat there, fingers entwined, the town of Fiesta dark and quiet outside the window of his candy store. Tomorrow, Cash could think about how being with Micah might affect his life. But for now, all he wanted was to feel his fingers linked in his, and watch his chest rise and fall as he took another breath.

Maybe, he thought, perhaps for the first time, *life is not what you plan for, but what you can't live without.*

Eleven

Micah slipped from Cash's bed, hating to leave the warmth of his new lover's side but restless and eager to continue on the mural. It had been days since he'd taken Cash's BJ virginity behind the counter of the Sweet Tooth but, tired from his grueling schedule in the Florida heat and eager to take it slow, they'd done little but cuddle and kiss ever since.

Now, well before dawn, he peered back from the doorway at Cash's sleeping form. His pale skin lingered in the powder blue sheets, body limp, dead to the world, his soft cotton boxers having slid down in the night to reveal the gentle curve of his left cheek. Micah smiled and, resisting temptation, slid the door shut with a soft click.

Exhaling slightly, he padded into the kitchen of Cash's cottage to brew a pot of coffee. The small, creaky bungalow felt so familiar to him by now, he hardly noticed himself reaching into the right cupboard for the mugs, the right drawer for a spoon, the right canisters for the creamer and sugar.

As he waited for the coffee to brew, Micah leaned against the counter, looking at the worn, comfy couch in the living room, a kind of battered, rust colored leather featuring orange, purple, and red throw pillows. A matching love seat boasted the same, though with a soft wheat colored throw tossed, just so, over the back and armrest.

The walls were a soft white and hung with ironic thrift shop beach scenes that, when taken together, were more kitschy and cool than anything else. Large windows were bordered by soft muslin curtains tied back with rough twine, the kind a fisherman might use. The coffee table was an old trunk with a round, chipped plate in the middle, covered with different shaped candles, wax pooled at their bottoms, and it was easy for Micah to picture Cash having a relaxing evening, feet up on the table, lost in a cozy mystery or torrid romance novel, a cup of jasmine tea by his side.

He sighed in contentment just looking at the rustic, cozy cottage; it was like some retired couple's second home and yet fit Cash's style perfectly. Calm, sedate, steady, mature, comfortable, the kind of place you couldn't wait to get home to every day, with the one person you couldn't wait to see.

His stomach fluttered as the coffee finished percolating. The mural was nearly through, not much more than a day or two left now to wrap it up and fill in the blanks. He'd expressly forbidden Cash to look at it and, to ensure his decree, had taken to hanging his paint spattered drop cloths up over the scaffolding atop which he worked every day, obscuring the progress so far.

Micah was worried what Cash might think of it when it was finished, but even more worried what he might do. After the mural was done, he reasoned, pouring himself a cup, what reason would he have to stick around?

Besides Cash, that is?

It was reason enough, to be sure, but sweaty midnight BJs behind the candy counter notwithstanding, Cash had made it clear he wasn't interested in living together as a couple. This arrangement was only temporary.

He sighed, sipping the strong brew and retreating to the guest room where he still kept his clothes. He dressed quickly—you couldn't wear much in the stifling heat—and grabbed a bagel from the fridge and his long board from the foyer on the way out the door.

It was still cool under the pale silver moon, and even more so once he bit into the bagel and slid his board on the front walk, sloping down the length of Seagull Lane with the breeze in his hair and soft on his skin.

This was how he liked Fiesta: dark, fragrant, breezy, and alone. Cash lived only a few blocks from his store and, in the predawn stillness, they flew by like picture postcard scenes.

Empty surf shops with winking lights around the windows, souvenir stands decked out in neon tank tops and endless flip flops, snow cone stands and ice cream parlors, bodegas and newsstands, all a dark blur as he munched the cinnamon raisin bagel and kept himself going with one foot occasionally reaching down to the pavement to speed himself along.

He rode down the middle of Ocean Drive, cruising from side to side, the world all to himself, the hum of the wheels beneath his feet and the crashing surf just beyond the only sounds in the world. Too soon the Sweet Tooth reared into view, with its quaint tropical storefront of yellow, green, and blue, its big plate glass windows, and, the only pockmark, Micah's scaffolding hidden beneath splotchy drop cloths.

He swerved through the alley, letting himself in the back delivery door with the key Cash had given him earlier in the week. Limber from the ride in, he stowed his long board in the stock room and grabbed a bottle of water from the break room fridge.

Still troubling over how to fit chocolate and lollipops into his concept—he'd already found a place for bubble gum and sugar plums and the rest of the store's most popular candy—he sank into Cash's desk chair and reached for a legal pad to flesh out an idea that had come to him earlier that morning.

He reached for the black marker resting on the edge of the desk but knocked it to the floor accidentally—all five of his fingers were obviously still asleep. He groaned, bending over to retrieve the elusive marker from between the edge of the desk and the wall.

He paused, finding a black frame resting in the breach. It was dusty from disuse and Micah was curious as to why it was resting on the floor beside Cash's desk and not hanging from the otherwise bare office wall. Sliding it free, he rested it atop his lap and nearly gasped when he recognized the artwork inside: it was the sketch he'd done of Cash, that final one from the last day of class their senior year.

Someone had gone to the trouble of framing it, centering the black and white sketch in white matting offset distinctly by the black metal frame. Micah had thought he'd never see it again, especially after leaving it in his room the night his father kicked him out for good.

So how the hell did it wind up in Cash's office? And what the hell was it doing on the fucking floor? Turning it over in search of clues, he saw a telltale scribble in the top right corner that solved the mystery immediately.

A note in his father's wobbly handwriting was scribbled on the tan backing of the frame:

Cash, I believe my son drew this of you. I know he would want you to have it and I hope you hang it in a place of honor, even if I couldn't. Yours, Ezra Taylor. PS: Sorry for the cheap frame!

Micah's face felt flushed, his heart pounding, blood rushing through his ears as he set the sketch down on Cash's desk. He stood abruptly, pacing the small office in fits and starts, shaking his head at the implications. He wondered at what point his father had put together that it was Cash in the sketch. The first time he'd walked into the Sweet Tooth? The second time? The third? The *last* time? Was that why he'd chosen to get his candy from the Sweet Tooth instead of the Discount Mart, or was it some random accident all the way around?

It didn't surprise him that his dad had framed one of his pieces. His father had been proud of Micah's art, once upon a time. Their house had always been filled with framed sketches and prints, watercolors, and self-portraits, whatever Micah had been into at the time. Hell, his father was the one who'd convinced him to go to art school in the first place, bugging him all senior year long to make sure he'd applied to all the top southern schools. Micah was only surprised that his father had framed *this* print—then gone to the trouble of giving it to Cash.

He could only imagine the scene, Ezra timid and shy, Cash confused and uncertain. And then… what? Cash had simply tossed it aside? Joked about it with his employees? Slid it between his office desk and the wall? Forgotten it altogether?

How else to explain the years' worth of dust that had piled up, the smeared glass and neglected hiding spot? What about it, he wondered, had made Cash discard it so callously?

He flushed a little at the obvious flattery. Cash's lean, angular face was bathed in an almost heroic light—hard to do with black and white and yet the effect was uncanny. His hair was shorter then, and Micah had made the eyes almost unrealistically big to reflect how much he liked to gaze into them. Whenever Cash wasn't looking, of course. Or whenever Micah could sneak a peek at him in the hallways or cafeteria, at his locker or in the gym. All in all, it was more an ode than a sketch, an obvious love letter to Cash's clean, flawless features. No wonder his father had reacted the way he had, so suddenly and callously. He might as well have kissed Cash right in front of him!

It was obviously drawn by someone smitten, in love, or at least lust, and he could see why Cash might have been embarrassed at first by the idealized portrait. But why hide it? It's not like Micah had ever signed it, and even if he had, who would ever look close enough to see?

And sure, maybe the black and white sketch in its austere white mat and black frame didn't exactly match the colorful candy posters in the store itself, but his office? He couldn't even hang it up where no one but the occasional cashier, delivery person, or stock boy might see it?

Micah had been so flattered by Cash's attention. From the first day he'd stumbled into the Sweet Tooth, Cash had been nothing short of breathless in his presence. That first night on the beach, the way he'd kissed Micah's lips and caressed his body in the surf, to say nothing of the way he'd tenderly caressed and serviced his cock, had been nothing short of… worshipful. In every passing glance and whispered kiss, every tender caress and powerful stroke, he had made it clear Micah was the answer to his dreams.

So why would he be too embarrassed to hang up his sketch? That is, unless, he was embarrassed of Micah himself?

He knew I loved him, Micah thought, admiring the sketch in all its adolescent glory. *He couldn't have looked at this drawing without realizing that. And yet he kept it hidden—not only from the world, but from himself. He's never going to be okay with us being together, not in the way I need him to. Openly and unashamed and fearless. And I can't stick around waiting for someone who is never going to love me the way I deserve to be loved.*

He slid the sketch atop the desk and promptly left the office. Left the stock room. Left the store. He had the presence of mind to grab his skateboard and lock up after himself, but that was the last rational thought he had for the next twelve hours.

Twelve

The day had taken its toll on Cash, body, mind, and soul. He'd risen not long after Micah, finding the coffee made, his mug laid out, and his lover long gone. He hadn't been far behind, eager to spend another day as close to Micah as possible—for as long as possible.

Sure, they'd be on the other side of a thick brick wall from each other, but the mere fact that they were a door away from one another brought Cash a sense of peace he'd never felt before—not even in his fantasies.

He'd sensed something was off the minute he unlocked the back door to the Sweet Tooth. The lights were on, but Micah's long board, an ever present fixture in the stock room since he'd arrived in Fiesta, was nowhere to be seen. Cash checked the break room, the bathroom, nothing. Then he popped his head in his office, and froze.

The sketch.

The damn sketch!

"Jesus," he murmured aloud, slumping into his desk chair and reaching for it. He blushed to stare at the idyllic image of himself, painted through the eyes of a schoolboy crush. It was embarrassingly beautiful, far more beautiful than he really was, and he remembered clearly the day Micah's father, Ezra, had brought it into the store with him.

It was his fourth or fifth visit, and Cash had looked up from the counter surprised to see him lugging in a large package wrapped in plain brown paper. He'd been in his uniform—tan work boots, forest green pants, and an olive green shirt bearing the Fiesta, Florida city logo.

Approaching cautiously, almost bashfully, he'd said, "You don't know me, Cash, but… I think you knew my son."

Cash had nodded, smiling. "Once upon a time," he'd said, that senior year seeming like a distant memory, even though only a few years had passed.

"Well, he obviously knew you," Ezra Taylor said, sliding the package atop the counter. "And I thought, well… I thought he'd want you to have this."

"What is it?" Cash had asked, heart racing with the mystery.

The old man had smirked and turned, already halfway toward the door. Hand on the knob, he'd turned and met Cash's eyes. Jutting out his chin proudly, he'd said, "It's priceless, is what it is. I just didn't know it at the time."

He'd left without another word and, eagerly, Cash unwrapped the gift. It was as beautiful then as it was now: Cash's face, sketched by someone clearly in love. He had studied every stroke and scratch, growled when the next customer came in.

Sliding the frame to the ground he'd waited on her, then six people more, until his part-timer at the time, a smartass high school kid named Phil, had come to relieve him—but not without checking out the sketch first.

"Damn!" he'd said, comparing the sketch with Cash's face side by side. "Someone loves you very, *very* much, boss."

Cash had blushed, yanked it from his hand, and, storming off, promptly hidden the sketch away so as to avoid further embarrassment. He'd wished he had the courage to hang it up, but knew he never would. If anyone ever found out who had drawn it, everything he'd worked so hard to build would be destroyed. After a while, he'd given up hopes of ever hanging it at work, but was reluctant to bring it home. He didn't have many visitors, but it only took one to find the adoring work of art in his guest room or den and realize what it meant and, more importantly, what it said about Cash that he kept it hanging around. Soon enough, he'd blocked the sketch from his mind completely.

That is, until he found it on his desk that morning. There was no doubt who'd found it—the artist himself. But where the hell had Micah gone?

Cash had texted him a dozen times in the hour before opening the store, then a dozen times since. He called him on his first break of the day, then at lunch, until, finally, he quit trying—and started searching.

"Frankie," he'd said to the part-timer behind the counter after lunch. "You're closing for me today. Got a problem with that?"

The kid had shrugged. "You're paying me overtime today. You got a problem with *that*?"

Any other day, Cash would have laughed at Frankie's cocky backtalk. Instead he shook his head grimly and turned, drifting through the swinging door and grabbing his long board from his office before bolting through the back delivery door.

Cash felt sick to his stomach as he launched his board on the sidewalk running parallel to Sunset Street and began to coast past the Sweet Tooth's neighboring businesses.

He probably should have hopped on the bike he kept locked up behind the store for daily errands or afternoon joyrides, or even leapt in his pickup truck to scour the small town of Fiesta in record time. But Micah's skateboard hadn't been at home or at the store and Cash knew he was either skating or on foot. The only way to track down a skater was to be a skater and that was one thing Cash and Micah had always shared.

Cash grunted as he rode through town, the sun warm on his back, wheels racing beneath him, shame flushing his face. How could he have been so stupid? How could he have ever let some random cashier, who had only worked for a few more weeks after his scathing comments, affect him in such a way that he would betray not only Ezra's trust in giving him the print, but Micah's for drawing it so tenderly in the first place?

No wonder Micah had bolted, leaving the sketch lying atop Cash's desk as a silent testament to the betrayal and the mural half finished—perhaps never to be completed at all. Cash would be lucky if he ever saw Micah again, let alone spoke to him.

Suddenly, it was all that mattered. Not the sniping remarks of some teenage cashier years earlier, not the sneering look from an old redneck's face across a diner counter, not even an entire town and what they might think. Nothing mattered if Micah spent another minute thinking Cash didn't appreciate the beautiful sketch—or his father's touching gesture.

The shame and fear drove him on, Cash stopping anywhere and everywhere he thought Micah might be. He started with the Art Mart, an irrational destination, to be sure, as if Micah might have bought a new sketchpad to draw Cash with horns on his head and a red complexion to match the devil he was.

But they hadn't seen him all day, nor had the folks at Sunshine Surf and Skate, where Cash had first bought the ragged long board he still rode to this day. Other than swimming up one lane and back again for the Fiesta High School swim team, Cash never been particularly athletic—to say nothing of coordinated. But when he saw Micah skating to school one day, Cash had gotten it into his head that perhaps they might bump into each other at the local skate park or on the way to school one sunny morning.

He'd spent the entire summer saving for his own board, even buying it at the same store as Micah had. Trying it out in the driveway on the last day of summer, Cash taken a harmless spill, sending the board flying into his mother's new Cadillac. She had been so incensed, she promptly took the board and hid it.

She'd hidden it so well, in fact, that it took Cash until Christmas break to find it wedged behind the wet vac in the garage. By then his attraction to Micah had grown so strong, he feared his knees would tremble if he ever skated in his presence and gave up on the idea of bumping into him altogether.

Instead he cruised up and down his own street, perfecting his moves—such as they were—in quiet silence, all the while imagining Micah at his side. Now he finally had what he wanted, right in his grasp, right in his own bed, the reality of their brief summer fling far surpassing even his wildest and most secret fantasies.

All shattered, all broken, because of pride. Not pride, Cash thought miserably as he skated through town, but fear. Fear of being outed, fear of being different, fear of gossip or bad press or whatever paranoid delusions he'd fancied during his years spent pining away for his artistic young lover. He was almost grateful to Gus and his rage for embodying his every fear and exposing it all at once.

There had been no need or time for the slow, gradual buildup of gossip and backstabbing to convince Cash that Micah had been right all along and that you would never be able to please all the people all the time. In one fell swoop, a man he'd spoken to nearly every day for years had shown the evil, prejudice, and hate lurking just beneath the surface.

How many other residents of Fiesta, how many more of his neighbors or customers or fellow grocery shoppers or moviegoers would react the same way if they saw Cash and Micah hand-in-hand, happier than they'd ever been? And why had it taken Cash so long to realize he no longer cared?

That wasn't necessarily true, he thought, skating past town and toward the only other place he thought Micah might go. It wasn't true that he didn't care. He *did* care that the people he thought he knew so well could care so little about his happiness that they would judge him on the very person that made him so happy.

But he cared about Micah so much more.

He had always fantasized about Micah in his life, yet those fantasies had been purely physical. Micah's hand in his own, their lips pressed against one another's, their bodies pressed against one another's, writhing in the night. The fantasies, however detailed, never once included a calm, quiet conversation, the kind they'd shared more often than kisses, hugs, or hand jobs in the week Micah had stayed at Cash's tiny cottage by the sea.

Now he knew how important both were to the man he loved, and how little the petty opinions of others suddenly meant. But how to convince Micah of all of that when it looked like the drawing he had so painstakingly created meant so little? How would Micah ever believe, let alone trust, Cash again?

He knew sweet and pretty words would not be enough, but he had no idea what might be. He only knew he had to find Micah before he left town and at least try to explain what life had been like in Fiesta without him. He only hoped it wasn't too late.

The cemetery was quiet and sprawling and he felt somehow disrespectful gliding along on his faithful old long board. He slowed to a stop and picked it up, walking past endless rows of graves until he arrived at Ezra's. It was humble and plain, a gift from the city of Fiesta, for which he had worked all his life. Micah was not there.

The spice drops were still there, however, safe and sound in a trademark green and white Sweet Tooth bag. He'd thought perhaps young vandals or hooligans might've absconded with the sack of savory treats, but maybe he'd just been watching too much TV lately.

There was a bench nearby, old and mossy and crumbling. The seat felt good beneath him, as he laid his skateboard down and laced his fingers together for a silent prayer in Ezra's honor.

They had never been a big churchgoing family, but he knew Ezra had been devout and figured… when in Rome. When he was done with his prayer, Cash stood to leave then abruptly sat back down. It was clear that Micah was already long gone. Or that even if he was still around, he wanted nothing to do with Cash. So what was his hurry?

Where did he have to go now that his heart had left him?

He looked at the grave and thought of what it must mean to lose a father. Divorce was one thing, but death was quite another. Worst came to worst, Cash knew he could still reach out to his father and hear his voice, maybe even hear a comforting word now that both of them had mellowed slightly with age. But death was permanent and, more than that, Ezra had died before Micah had had a chance to find closure.

Perhaps if Micah had come home a little sooner or Ezra had given the drawing back to his son instead of Cash, things might've been different. But now Micah was alone. There was an aunt somewhere, but clearly they weren't very close if it had taken her weeks to track him down in the first place. Cash didn't know much about Micah's mother save for the fact that she'd been white and had passed away when he was still a boy. Cancer or emphysema, he wasn't sure which, only that it had been Ezra and Micah for as long as anyone could remember, and then only Ezra once he kicked Micah out for good.

Now all Micah had was a donated grave marker and a tired old bench on which to sit if he wanted to visit his old man. It made the sting of Cash's betrayal all the more savage, he thought. Not to put words in Micah's mouth or emotions in his heart, but Cash couldn't help but think that Micah's sad homecoming had been softened somewhat by his presence. That his fateful trip to the Sweet Tooth had meant something to both of them, and not just Cash. That they'd both trembled and shaken with forbidden desire and pent-up emotion that first time they kissed in the moonlit sea. That Cash had been a familiar face and a soft place to land when Micah came home an orphan.

To spend a week in endless bliss only to discover that Cash had orphaned him as well must've been the final straw for poor Micah. Cash shook his head, realizing it had been a fool's errand to try and find him in the first place. Cash stood in front of Ezra's grave, clutching his board and bowing his head.

"I'm sorry, Ezra," he said, voice tired and out of breath. Not from skating all around town, but from the sudden emotions that threatened to cripple him. "I'm sorry I didn't appreciate the gift you gave me. I'm sorry I let others shame me into hiding it. I'm sorry I let your boy down. I promise that I'll hang it up with pride. I promise that I'll live with pride. Because everyone deserves to be proud of who they are. You deserved to be proud of your boy, and he deserved to be proud of his art. I'm only sorry I did so little when you finally saw fit to give it to me. I said 'thank you' that day, but I mean it now and I hope you rest in peace knowing that someone still loves your son. Knowing that he's not an orphan as long as I'm alive to know how special he is and how stupid I was to ever let him go."

Cash turned from the grave, thinking how if this had been a movie Micah would've been standing there, grinning ear to ear and wiping a glycerin tear from his ebony cheek. Instead the cemetery was as quiet and deserted as it was when he entered and he left on foot, carrying his board until just past the cemetery gate. Then he slid it onto the long, snaking driveway and skated back toward town. There were no pit stops this time; no detours. He stomped his foot and sped toward home, wanting nothing more than a cold shower to wipe the sweat from his body and hide the tears from himself.

The sun was sinking low now, the picture postcard town of Fiesta looking as scenic and tropical as ever. He cruised down Seagull Lane, hands behind his back, both feet on the board, letting the gradual decline draw him toward home. The cottage looked perfect and sterile in its quiet emptiness. Micah was right about one thing: Cash *had* created the perfect life for himself.

The perfect job, the perfect store, the perfect cottage with the perfect palms and landscaping and wide front porch where he rested his skateboard as he always did, atop one of the two Adirondack chairs in which he never sat. The door was locked, dashing his last hope that Micah might have let himself in to give Cash one last chance to redeem himself.

Instead he walked in his house alone, shutting the door behind him and grabbing a beer from the fridge. The shower could wait, he decided. For now he just wanted to sit on the back deck and gaze at the ocean where he and Micah had shared their first kiss and he, at least, had fallen hopelessly—even recklessly—in love.

Wherever Micah had gone, Cash hoped that whenever he looked at the sea he would at least think of Cash in the crashing waves and frothy surface, for that was how Cash would always look to the sea from here on in.

He heard the reggae halfway to the sliding glass door and, pausing, saw the glint of Micah's cell phone on the weathered table between the faded deck chairs. He sat in the left one, as he always did, and didn't turn when Cash hesitantly slid open the sliding glass door. Cash paused, heart pounding with relief, wearing an uncertain expression as he crept closer. *Will Micah be irate?* he wondered. *Has he stuck around just to chew me out? Or is he here… to stay?*

"Took you long enough," Micah said, waving an empty beer bottle. Cash sank into the empty seat and handed him his beer. He no longer needed it anyway. His heart was pounding, cells flooded with adrenaline as he wondered what might happen next.

Thirteen

"Where have you been?" Cash asked.

He looked flushed, flustered, even panicked as he sat in the weathered Adirondack chair and then promptly stood back up again.

Micah waved his beer, taking in the back deck, the scruffy dunes, and the pounding waves below. "Right here."

Cash looked incredulous. "The whole time?"

"Well, not the *whole* time," he confessed, smirking as Cash swiped his beer and took a healthy swallow before handing it back. "I mean, I had to wait till your sorry ass was gone."

Cash's face fell, as if he'd forgotten why they'd been apart all day in the first place. Micah noted his flushed face, sweaty armpits, and breathless voice. "Why, where have *you* been?"

Cash paused while pacing back and forth across the deck to give him another look of shock and awe. "Looking for you, what the fuck do you think?"

Micah waited until Cash was in range to swipe his beer back. "I'm flattered, Cash. But you didn't have to do that."

"Of course I did," Cash insisted. "I wanted to find you. I *had* to find you, to tell you how sorry I am."

Micah waved a hand, which just happened to be the one with the beer in it. Cash grabbed it on the upswing and nearly finished it in one swig.

"Look," he said, mellow from the peaceful hours of restful meditation on Cash's back deck, the sun caressing his skin, the crashing waves lulling him into a state of forgiveness he hadn't felt when he first sat down earlier that day. "I was wrong to storm off like that. I should've hung around and talked it out. I just… that picture was the last thing I saw before Dad kicked me out. You know? I think more than his gravestone, it made me realize he's really gone. I took it out on you and I shouldn't have."

This time the look on Cash's face was actual shock. "I hid a picture that you drew of me out of love," he blurted, as if disappointed that he'd been forgiven so easily. "That your father gave to me, out of respect. I diss you both and *you're* apologizing to *me*?"

Micah shrugged. "I'm not saying what you did was right. I'm just saying that what I did wasn't right, either."

All the fight seemed to go out of Cash then, as he handed the rest of the beer back to Micah before slumping down in the chair beside him.

"When I found that sketch this morning, I saw red, Cash. I ran away. There's no other word for it. I thought you hated me, like my father hated me—"

"He didn't hate you, Micah," Cash interrupted.

Micah squeezed his hand, hard. "I think I only have the strength to say this once, Cash. So please… let me say it quickly?"

Cash nodded.

"I thought you hated me, so I ran. I skated out to the edge of town, wearing just the clothes on my back, figuring I'd hitch a ride to somewhere. Anywhere. But nobody picks up black guys these days, especially in Fiesta. But I'm lucky, because… as I sat there, thumb out, flicking off everybody who sped on by, I realized… I don't want to go and do graphics design for some advertising agency down in South Beach. I would be miserable there too, if I had to spend every day without you. I have no interest in any future that you're not going to be in."

Micah paused, winded. He'd been rehearsing the speech all day so that, by the time he actually gave it, he was worn out.

Cash smiled, eyes moist.

Micah took Cash's hand. "I came back was because I knew that anywhere else but here would make me miserable. I'm tired of being miserable, Cash. I want to be happy for a change. You make me happy. You always have. That's… that's why I drew that picture in the first place."

Cash stood abruptly. "Let's go," he said, tugging Micah to his feet. "Let's go and hang it up in the store right now."

Micah gripped his hand, squeezing it tight. "You don't have to do that, Cash. I couldn't even give you that sketch myself, I was so ashamed. I can't blame you for being ashamed of it—"

"I was never ashamed of it!" Cash blurted, cutting him off. "Never, Micah. I just… I'm a pussy, I guess. I'm afraid, or I was, of what people might think. I thought they might know you drew it of me, that a boy did, and I chose them over my love for you. I can't… I won't do that again, Micah."

"I don't want you to change for me, Cash," Micah murmured, inching closer to smell the sun and heat and sweat on Cash's skin.

"I'm not," he insisted, hands drifting apart to slide on either side of Cash's waist. "I'm changing with you. There's a difference. One you do to get someone. The other you do to keep him. I don't want to lose you again. I don't want to lose you *ever*."

Micah smiled and reached for his hand across the small space between their chairs. It felt soft and warm and right. "That's good," he said, squeezing Cash's fingers. "Because I don't ever want to get lost again."

Cash squeezed back, hard. "You mean…"

Micah leaned forward to kiss Cash's full, damp lips, the feeling electric and warm, as always. "Just try getting rid of me," he murmured as they sank into one another.

Cash was resolute, and dragged himself away. "Come with me," he insisted, tugging Micah inside. "Let's go, right now, and pick out a good place for your picture."

They got as far as the living room before Micah made his stand. "Maybe later, Cash. Maybe… tomorrow."

Cash cocked his head. "Why not now?"

Micah smirked. "Because I've got other plans for you tonight, Cash. Plans for us."

"Yeah?"

Micah tugged him down the hall toward the guest room, where the moon had been shining inside his room for the last three nights straight. "I want to lie next to you, Cash," he said, dragging him inside the moonlit room. "I want to be with you."

Cash stood inside the room, skin still sweaty and aglow in the streaks of moonlight streaming in through the open window. A soft breeze rustled the orange curtains on either side, just above the double bed with its soft white sheets.

"I want to be inside you," Micah tempted, feeling Cash's pulse quicken as they stood, face to face, hand in hand in the middle of the room. "Are you ready for that?"

Cash merely nodded, licking his full, thick lips. "If you are," he said.

Micah smirked, reaching for the hem of Cash's Sweet Tooth shirt. "I've been ready since the day I got back into town, Cash. I've been ready since that night on the beach. I've been ready since that night behind the candy counter. I've been ready since I got back here, hours ago. I'll never be more ready, Cash, and no one will ever love you more than I do."

Cash gulped, literally, and dutifully lifted his arms above his head. Large, round areolas surrounded stiff nipples, twitching as Micah bent to kiss and lick them clean.

Cash was a live wire, trembling openly as Micah undressed him tenderly until he stood, fat cock curved downward as it hardened, ginger bush unruly and thick as Micah ran his ebony fingers through its wispy stretches before gripping him tight.

"We'll take it slow," he promised, taking his lover in hand and stroking him gently as he peppered his blushing ear with butterfly kisses. "We've got all night, we've got forever, Cash, and when you come, it will change your life…"

Cash turned his head to kiss him, feverish and hungry as his cock stiffened, slick and damp in Micah's gentle grip. "It already has," he whispered, breath hot as their lips mingled. "My life changed the minute you walked through that door last week. And I knew…" His breath hitched as Micah led him to the bed. "I knew I'd never be the same."

Micah nodded, laying him down in the soft white sheets, his body bathed in silver light. If only Micah had his sketchpad handy, he'd trade it all for the chance to record this moment forever. Then again, he knew, kicking off his shoes and tugging off his shirt, this would be a night neither of them would ever forget.

Fourteen

Micah slid off his shirt. He looked flawless, as ever, and Cash propped himself up on one elbow to watch the show. A soft breeze caressed his skin, failing to cool him as Micah's lean frame and wiry muscles heated up the room a good ten degrees.

He slid off his shorts, boxers sliding down his waist in the process. He paused, only a moment, their eyes meeting in the shimmering silver darkness. Then he tugged them down, freeing his thick cock and awakening things in Cash he'd never felt before.

Micah stood, as if uncertain where to go next, but Cash merely crooked a finger and propped on his side at the edge of the bed, licking his lips suggestively. Micah smirked and had but to take a step or two forward for Cash to take him in his mouth. His mouth was molten and wet, and he could feel it seizing around the tip of Micah's cock and embracing it like a glove fits a fist.

He'd only meant to taste it, to nibble it, to tease it, but one taste of his lover's thick, veiny flesh made him wanton with longing. He slid his legs around, planting his feet on the floor, one on either side of Micah's right thigh. He breathed through his nose, heart pounding with desire, with the realization that this night, at last, after twenty-two years, he would lie with another man.

But not just any man: Micah. The knowledge made him passionate and frenzied and, hands sliding around his lover's waist, Cash gripped each round, perfect cheek and squeezed, eliciting a gasp and sigh as Micah inched deeper inside Cash's clingy lips.

They remained right there, neither of them moving except for Cash's tongue, probing his lover's meaty staff and his lips sucking the top half and savoring the liquid heat that surrounded it. Micah murmured and squirmed but never thrust or ground himself deeper. Instead he let them linger there, Cash's fingers dug deep in his lover's ass, caressing and rubbing and kneading them until Micah murmured, "I'm clean, if you're wondering. Got my test results before I left Atlanta, so…"

Cash made a game of answering him, sucking and licking teasingly before gasping, "I trust you, Micah. And I've never been with… anyone… so…"

Then his mouth returned to its subtle, erotic rhythm, making Micah whimper and squirm and tremble in reply.

When at last neither of them could resist any longer, Micah croaked, "I'm so wet, baby. Let me love you now…"

Cash nodded, dragging his lips along Micah's staff until it glistened and shone in the moonlight. Then, without another word, he lay back down, flat this time, on his belly, his own dick hard and damp in the cheap white sheets.

"Not like that," Micah murmured, sliding onto the bed beside him. "I don't want to pound you, I want to make love to you. Here…" He helped Cash back onto his side, facing the wall, Micah sliding in to fill the space at his back, as if they were spooning. "Isn't that better?"

Cash was afraid to speak, for fear his voice might tremble and give away the soft, damp tears that caressed his feverish cheeks. Micah gripped his shoulder gently, squeezing it reassuringly as Cash trembled in his arms. With the other hand he guided his slick, swollen tip toward the space between Cash's cheeks, tender and tight and new. He could feel the dampness and the heat, and that was before Micah licked his fingers and slid them toward the tight, puckered hole that flinched and spasmed at the touch. Warm and wet, Micah took it slowly, sliding a gentle fingertip in, then out, as Cash gently murmured and moaned with want.

Another finger joined the first as Cash gripped the sheets tightly with one hand, the other pressed against the wall as Micah moved him gently forward, then back, with every gentle thrust and glide deeper inside. Hot breath washed across his bare shoulders, clashing with the gentle sea breeze as Micah grew desperate with desire.

His fingers slid from inside Cash's tight sheath and were quickly replaced by the swollen, leaking tip of Micah's staff. It was feverishly hot and, despite his virginity, Cash leaned back into it, eager to feel that swollen heat glide deep inside. It didn't take long; his sphincter dampened and stretched by Micah's fingers, puckered and yawning as the tip slid just inside. There was a slight vacuum "pop" of pressure; Cash gasped and gripped the wall as momentum dragged another inch, then two more, deeper inside.

Micah paused with his chest pressed against Cash's back, fingers gripping his shoulder tight as he murmured, "This okay?"

Cash could merely nod, biting down on his lip to squeal in delight at the bittersweet combination of pleasure and pain that made his own cock throb and leak as it lay amidst the damp, twisted sheets.

Without another word, Micah slid deeper inside, Cash gasping, breathless with anticipation until at last he felt his lover's pelvis flush with the round bubble of his ass.

Wedged deep inside, bodies connected, skin to skin, Micah slid both arms around Cash's sides until they wrapped around his waist. Only then, tenderly and achingly, did he begin to gently thrust his hips to drag and drift from the tight, damp hole before gliding just back inside.

It was a tender rhythm, Cash breathless with delight, stuffed deep and speechless as he began to feel the tip of Micah's staff press against some unseen button that, with each gentle thrust, brought a fresh drop of icing from the tip of his cock and his throbbing climax closer to the surface.

Lying on their sides, skin flush with sweat, the curtains rustling above their heads, Micah began to grind himself deeper, thrust himself harder, panting eloquently along the back of Cash's neck as he felt his lover's climax approaching.

His grip tightened around Cash's belly, drawing him even closer just as Micah plunged deeper. With a gasp and a pulsing throb he came, wet lust spilling deep inside as the sensation triggered in Cash a sympathetic response. His cock spat and sputtered into the twisted sheets, Cash trembling with surprise and ecstasy as he whimpered into the pillow beneath his face, powerless to stop the emotions and physical tremors that raced through his body.

They lay like that, bodies wedged tightly together, long after both had grown limp and Micah had slid from inside the virgin walls, virgin no more. Cash could feel Micah's heart still pounding, long after their jizz had started to dry and the moon danced along the late night sky. Safe in his lover's arms, Micah's hands still clinging tightly around his trembling belly, Cash drifted into a dreamless sleep.

Fifteen

Micah stood nervously as the tarps he'd rigged the night before slid gently down the far side of the Sweet Tooth. Cash stood by his side, shifting from foot to foot nervously as the mural was at last revealed.

It was just after dawn a few days later, neither of them able to sleep and eager to have the mural unveiled and visible before the store opened a few hours later. Breathlessly, Micah turned from the wall to find Cash, mouth agape, eyes wide, inching gently forward.

"You hate it, don't you?" Micah murmured, following him until Cash was close enough to reach out and touch the wall.

"Is it safe?" he asked, ignoring Micah's expression of self-doubt. "To touch the paint, I mean?"

Micah nodded, watching Cash gently drag his fingertips along one of the rainbow beams as his full lips curved into a smile. "Where did you come up with this idea?" he asked, stepping back to admire it anew.

Micah followed him. "Just sitting in the park one day," he confessed, thinking how long ago that fateful day felt.

Trying to see the mural through Cash's eyes, he stood by his lover's side to admire it objectively. It began simply enough, a candy jar toward the left bottom of the wall, as if resting on the pavement. It was filled with all sorts of sweets, licorice and gum drops, chocolate and lemon sours, lollipops, and bubble gum. From the open lid of the jar, a rainbow sprouted, shooting up and over and down, toward the right, ending just along the far side of the building closest to Sunshine Street.

Dancing across the bands of the colorful rainbow, vibrant and bright, ran happy pairs of chubby, idealized children: a little white boy and a little brown girl held hands as they skipped along the bright blue band, a brown girl and a tan girl held hands and skipped along the yellow beam, a white boy and a black boy clung to one another, fingers clasped, as they ran across the green beam. Frolicking together, they licked lollipops or chomped on candy bars, smiling and happy and free. As if inspired by the mural, Cash reached out to gently clasp Micah's fingers. He wasn't sure if it was in consolation, as he was about to fire him, or simply an impromptu act of romantic goodwill. Either way, he had never felt anything so right in all his life.

Micah had no idea how long he'd been gazing at the mural, lost in the subtle little nuances of a candy wrapper or a child's hand, one of his father's favorite spice drops or the swirls in a lollipop, until he heard murmurs behind him.

Turning, slowly, Micah realized other shopkeepers had emerged from their stores, standing in aprons or cloaks, converging in tight little clusters of two or three people, merged with bystanders who'd just been casually cruising down the street.

He heard murmurs and saw admiring glances, suddenly realizing they had an audience; and a sizable one at that. His face burned with nervousness, and he expected Cash to feel the same, but when Micah squeezed Cash's hand playfully, Cash merely turned to acknowledge the growing assemblage.

Micah had expected Cash to flee, to run, to blush or break out in a cold sweat, or try to dig clear into the asphalt to avoid the implications of not only a gay-friendly mural but a clearly affectionate artist, one whose hand he was still holding.

Instead he began to greet members of the crowd by name. "Hi, Sheila," he murmured to a woman who worked at Brioche next door, waving with his free hand while clinging to Micah's with the other. "What do you think of the mural?"

"It's great," said the middle-aged woman in the cherry red apron. "Is this the artist?"

Cash nodded proudly, raising Micah's hand up like a prizewinning fighter after a heavyweight bout. "Micah did it. He's super talented!" he bragged.

Micah felt like a student being manhandled by his stage mother, jostled about from cluster to cluster until at last Cash had polled nearly every bystander in the crowd rapidly growing in the alley beside the mural.

"Hi, Gus," Cash finally said, pointedly, to a withered old man standing alone on the curb. "What do you think of Micah's mural?"

The old man snuffed and nodded begrudgingly. "It shows… promise," he confessed, before a group of giggling waitresses in pink aprons scolded him playfully and the single detractor was silenced. Micah felt bathed in warmth, and not just from the rising sun.

Perhaps he'd been wrong about tiny Fiesta, Florida, all this time. Maybe it did have potential, after all. Maybe they weren't out to get him, or Cash, for falling in love. Maybe, just maybe, there was hope for them—and the town—yet.

"So?" Micah asked, ignoring the crowd murmuring at their back and playfully choking an answer out of Cash. "Forget what *they* think. Do you like it or do I have to paint it black and start from scratch?"

"Don't you dare!" Cash gasped, shrugging off his hands. "I love it, every inch of it. I just… it's so much more than what I expected."

"What did you expect?"

"Like, a big tooth or something. You know? Because of… Sweet Tooth?"

Micah rolled his eyes so hard he almost got a headache. "Give me a little more credit than that, okay?"

Cash chuckled and, right there, in the light of a new day, wrapped him in a warm, gentle hug. He even kissed him, with the crowd at his back and everything. And no one screamed. Or picketed. Or pelted them with rotten tomatoes and eggs. No one made a sound but, instead, began to gently disperse, as if sensing a private moment had just occurred.

"Careful, Tiger," Micah had to warn him, pushing him away playfully as a few in the crowd offered nervous twitters in response to the public display of affection. "This is a family store, remember? Let's take it in off the street if you're going to get frisky."

Cash frowned, admiring the mural once more. "What? I thought we'd stand here staring at this all day!"

"It's yours, Cash. Remember? You paid for it."

Cash settled for holding hands as they watched the rising sun cast shadows across the sweeping mural. "About that," he said, squeezing Micah's hand. "Now that the mural's done, I thought... we might talk about your future here at the Sweet Tooth organization."

They drifted away then, toward the back entrance, shutting the door behind them and drifting closer for a soft, chaste kiss before following each other into the store proper.

"You have something else for me to paint?" Micah teased, leaning against one of the high, bistro style tables that lined the front store window.

"Alas, no. But school will be starting soon and I always lose half my part-time help the first week of August. I thought, if you wouldn't mind bagging up gum drops and lollipops with me all day, you might be a good fit."

Micah's heart did a little flutter. "Are you sure? I mean, you, me, together all day?"

Cash pretended to be offended. "You got a problem with that?"

"Just one," Micah purred, inching closer to the sales counter, behind which Cash still stood. "How are we going to keep our hands off each other?"

"Who says we have to?" Cash chuckled, both of them leaning across the counter for a kiss. "I mean, anytime we get randy, I'll just turn the 'Open' sign over to 'Closed' and we're good to go."

"Could impact sales, though…" Micah mused playfully, peering over Cash's shoulder to where a new frame, black bordered with a white mat, hung amidst a smattering of children's movie posters. Inside, the sketch he'd done of Cash during senior year hung, freshly polished and gleaming.

"Naw," Cash said, turning to admire the sketch as well. "I've got a loyal fan base. They'll wait a few minutes to get their sugar fix."

"A few minutes?" Micah chuckled, sliding onto—then over—the bright red counter. "When have you ever lasted that long?"

Cash blushed, their bodies sliding together like two puzzle pieces in the tight space behind the counter. "Can I help it if you get me all hot and bothered?"

"I suppose not," Micah murmured between stolen kisses that grew hotter and heavier with each glancing blow. "So which are you now … hot or bothered?"

Cash grabbed his hand, tugging him toward the swinging half-door. "Why don't you take me in the stock room and find out?"

Micah chuckled at Cash's cockiness, finding it suited him. "I guess I *should* get more familiar with the place," he murmured, following closely behind. "Seeing as I'll be working here now…"

"Thank god I never put that whole 'no sleeping with the boss' thing on the application, or the next few minutes would be really awkward."

"Try the next few seconds," Micah murmured before sealing Cash's lips shut with a soft, tender kiss that turned into something much, much more.

A Sneak Peek from Crimson Romance
Nothing's Sweeter than Candy
by Lotchie Burton

Candace Brown stood in the hotel lobby staring at the row of elevators, hesitant to push the button that would take her to the upper levels. Nash, her once-in-a-blue-moon lover had called. He'd said he was in town, but only for the night. Her "if you had any sense" inner voice had shrieked *bad idea* as soon as she'd hung up the phone. But every woman alive knows raging hormones and no sex for months will kick a sensible thought in its ass, and trample it right into the dust.

She'd rushed out the door, jumped in her car, and driven there at breakneck speed, ready for a long-overdue romp between the sheets. Now with only an elevator ride standing between her and satisfying the ache between her legs, that nagging voice reemerged and refused to be ignored. And it told her she was about to take stupid to a whole other level. Suddenly she was undecided.

In the few months she'd known him, he'd never shown a capacity to care about other human beings or feel real emotion. There wasn't a sensitive, civilized bone in his body. Lately, he'd started the annoying habit of calling her "Freak." He claimed it was a term of endearment, but the unpleasant way the word rolled off his tongue felt more like accusation than kindness. She loathed the way it made her feel. Nash enjoyed using offensive, demeaning language to make her uncomfortable and feel less like a woman and more like an object.

Basically, Andrew Nash was an asshole. He'd weaseled his way into her life using his affable charm, a trait she'd quickly learned was pure gimmick. Her first mistake was agreeing to go out with him, immediately followed by her second: going to bed with him.

And she'd continued falling into bed with him again and again, all while ignoring her better judgment and ditching her sense of pride.

So why did she keep coming back? Because he was handsome and fit, and in spite of his asinine behavior, the man knew his way around a woman's body. His hands and mouth flowed like pure magic over every inch of her—pushing her buttons, plucking her cords, and playing her like a fine-tuned instrument. Aware of his abilities and her weaknesses, he skillfully used both to manipulate her and turn her inside out. When she was with him, she *was* the freak he'd named her—he knew exactly how to make her lose control. It pissed her off that the man who let loose her deepest inhibitions took such great pleasure in mocking her for it.

The fact that Candace's lust for Nash far outweighed her self-respect hadn't mattered until now. So what had changed? Why hadn't she pushed that elevator button? Maybe she'd finally grown tired of his demeaning comments and deliberate disrespect. Maybe the sex wasn't worth the insults. Maybe it was time to stop settling for temporary satisfaction while enduring constant humiliation. While struggling to make her choice, she was distracted by her reflection in the highly polished chrome of the elevator doors. The sight stirred up a startling memory; the walls and sounds of the lobby melted away, replaced by a more powerful and provoking image.

All of a sudden she was with Nash, standing before a long bank of windows as high as the ceiling, staring back at their reflection in the tinted sheets of glass. The world beyond was muted and shrouded in darkness, illuminated solely by pinpoints of artificial light that flickered in distant windows or flashed by in the street way down below. The room was nearly as dark, dimly lit with soft lighting that spilled over from an adjacent room. Their naked bodies were cast in silhouette and posed on full display in front of the window, where they stood uncaring and unashamed.

She leaned back and relaxed her body into his, her hips and thighs cradled against him. She gave in to the tingling sensations created by caressing hands that glided over her sensitive skin in long, sensual strokes. Hands that swept across her shoulders, down her back, and reached underneath her breasts, cupping and lifting them high. Molded around her full and swaying flesh, his fingers pulled and pinched her distended nipples hard, sending electrical shivers down her spine. Warm, moist breath pushed through her curls and tantalized her ear and neck. His wet tongue probed her ear and teased her neck and throat, seeking the soft, telltale sounds of pleasure as proof that she craved his touch.

He pressed her tightly against him, fusing them together and pulling her back against his stiff arousal. The coarse hairs on his thighs and pelvis chafed against the soft skin of her bare back and bottom, the friction tormenting her. He bent her forward doggy-style in front of the window and moved his body seductively over hers, rubbing against her entrance before easing his stiff length into her waiting wetness. They shared the titillating sensation of penetration, the electrifying feeling of his steel sliding through her satin. Their bodies quivered in pleasure from the intimate joining, his cock encircled by her liquid heat.

Immersed in the moment, they wordlessly watched their bodies in motion, reflected in the glass. She saw through half-closed lids the paleness of his white skin against her darker complexion, and shuddered as his shaft moved with a slow, steady rhythm, in and out between her slick, silken folds. Together they moved in one fluid motion like partners in a private dance, pulling apart and meeting in the middle with force and fervor, again and again. Overcome by nearly unbearable sensations, she alternately welcomed the pleasure and fought against the building ache that would too soon take her over the edge. Fiery heat poured through her veins and scorched and burned her from the inside. The warmth surged and bubbled up into her throat as she soared inevitably toward climax, and emerged as the sound a woman makes on the verge of losing control.

His pace quickened and became more forceful. He pulled her up and pushed her hard against the window and pressed her face and breasts into the glass, her arms splayed out to her sides. Her back arched deeper and her legs spread wider to accommodate his furious and repeated plunges inside her velvet channel. She was lost in passion, overcome by sensation. Approaching the edge of his climax, he grabbed a handful of her hair, yanked her head back, and wrapped his arm around her waist. He pulled her down and pounded her again and again with his thrusting cock. His fingers unerringly found her throbbing clit and furiously rubbed against her sensitive flesh until she erupted in an orgasm so strong she staggered and nearly crumpled to the floor ...

The buzzing sound of her phone vibrating in her purse interrupted her brief, yet vivid recollection. The caller ID told her it was Nash.

"Hello?"

"Hey, Freak. I've been waiting for over an hour. Where are you?"

Her jaw tightened. Instant clarity flooded her indecisive mind, and common sense demanded to be heard. There wasn't a damn thing between her and Nash except hot sex. They weren't even friends. Their "relationship" was purely physical and based on convenience for her and mockery for him. Suddenly she realized that being the object of ridicule for the sake of good sex was *ridiculous*.

A dull red shade of anger spread across her cheeks. This was it. This was her wakeup call. She wasn't taking any more crap from Andrew Nash, no matter how good he was in bed.

"I'm not coming."

"You're not coming? Yeah, right." He laughed in sarcastic disbelief. "That's a good one, Freak. So where are you?" he continued. "The nights a-wasting, and I've got plans for that freaky brown-sugar ass of yours."

"I said I'm not coming. I'm not taking any more of your shit. You may be a good fuck, Nash, but that's the only 'good' thing about you. I'm ending this while I still have some of my dignity intact. Sorry for the short notice, but I know you won't have any trouble replacing me with some other freak."

"Look, Freak, I'm not in the mood for games." His voice took on an angry edge. "Get your ass over here. If you keep me waiting too long, I might have to spank that pretty brown ass, just to teach you a lesson."

The mere mention of the promised spanking made her weak in the knees. A gush of liquid desire soaked her underwear—and pissed her off even more.

"You're an asshole, Nash," she hissed through clenched teeth.

"Yeah, I know." He laughed harshly. "But you're gonna show. We both know you're a fucking addict, and I'm your drug."

Candace viciously stabbed the "end call" button on her phone, walked swiftly back toward the hotel entrance, and gave the valet her ticket. Still fuming when her car arrived, she handed the young man a generous tip and silently celebrated her small victory by charging the parking fee to the asshole's room.